Smith's
MONTHLY

Every Month Original Novels, Stories, and Articles

USA Today Bestselling Writer
Dean Wesley Smith

TABLE OF CONTENTS

SHORT STORIES

FULL NOVEL

NONFICTION

SMITH'S MONTHLY ISSUE #44

All Contents copyright © 2017 Dean Wesley Smith
Published by WMG Publishing
Cover and interior design copyright © 2017 WMG Publishing
Cover art copyright © by Joseph Golby/Dreamstime.com

"Introduction: Sometimes I Worry Myself" © 2017 by Dean Wesley Smith.

"A Look at His Heart: A Marble Grant Story" © 2017 by Dean Wesley Smith, cover and layout copyright © 2017 by WMG Publishing.

"Wings Out: A Bryant Street Story" © 2017 by Dean Wesley Smith, cover and layout copyright © 2017 by WMG Publishing

"Keep Hoping for a New Tomorrow" © 2017 by Dean Wesley Smith, cover and layout copyright © 2017 by WMG Publishing.

"The Wait" © 2017 by Dean Wesley Smith, cover and layout copyright © 2017 by WMG Publishing.

Burn Card: A Cold Poker Gang Novel © 2017 by Dean Wesley Smith, Published by WMG Publishing, Cover and layout copyright © 2017 by WMG Publishing, cover art copyright © by Joseph Golby | Dreamstime.

Heinlein's Rules: Five Simple Business Rules for Writing, A WMG Writer's Guide © 2017 by Dean Wesley Smith, cover and layout copyright © 2017 by WMG Publishing.

This book is licensed for your personal enjoyment only. All rights reserved.
This is a work of fiction. All characters and events portrayed in the fiction in this book are
fictional, and any resemblance to real people or incidents is purely coincidental.
This book, or parts thereof, may not be reproduced in any form without permission.

Introduction to Issue #44
Sometimes I Worry Myself

Every writer I know feels that worry at times if the writer is writing from the creative voice. And that is all I ever write from, without a thought of censoring myself in any way.

I never outline.

I never know where I am going with a story.

I just write to entertain myself as if I am a reader of the story as I type it and I hope in the process I entertain you as well.

So in July, as part of a novel challenge, I wrote a Cold Poker Gang novel called *Burn Card*. It is the novel in this issue.

When I started into the book, I had no idea what it would be about. Not one clue. I just knew it would be my retired detectives solving a cold case. Didn't even know what the crime would be.

But I did have a short story with the two detectives that I had written about how some cold cases turn out to be very simple to solve, even after thirty years of being cold.

So I took that short story and asked the question. "Maybe not? What happens if that case in the short story hadn't been so easy?"

And off I went typing.

Suddenly bodies started to appear. More and more bodies.

And other ugly things that humans do to each other that I won't detail here because I don't want to spoil the novel read for you.

I had no idea about any of it. I just kept writing as my detectives dug deeper and deeper.

So now, as I went back to put this issue together, I looked at *Burn Card* again and had that writer worry about how I could come up with that sort of stuff.

Ugly stuff.

Yet I know all writers often worry about the same thing. I am no different at all.

In this issue there is a Marble Grant short story right after this introduction.

Thanks for the Support

Dean Wesley Smith

Marble Grant has quickly become one of my favorite characters and I honestly have no idea where the stuff Marble does comes from either.

But I sure love writing her stories.

So you want to see the same writer on opposite extremes of writing, read the Marble Grant story, then read the twisted mystery novel *Burn Card*.

Both came out of the same brain within a month of each other.

And I had not one ounce of control over either story. I just went along for the ride and typed as fast as I could to get the story on the page, entertaining myself as I went along.

I hope you are as entertained by both stories and the others in this issue as I was writing them.

—*Dean Wesley Smith*
August 22nd, 2017

Can't Get Enough of Marble Grant?
These stories and more are available at your favorite booksellers.

Coming Next Issue in *Smith's Monthly*

MARBLE GRANT
A Marble Grant Novel

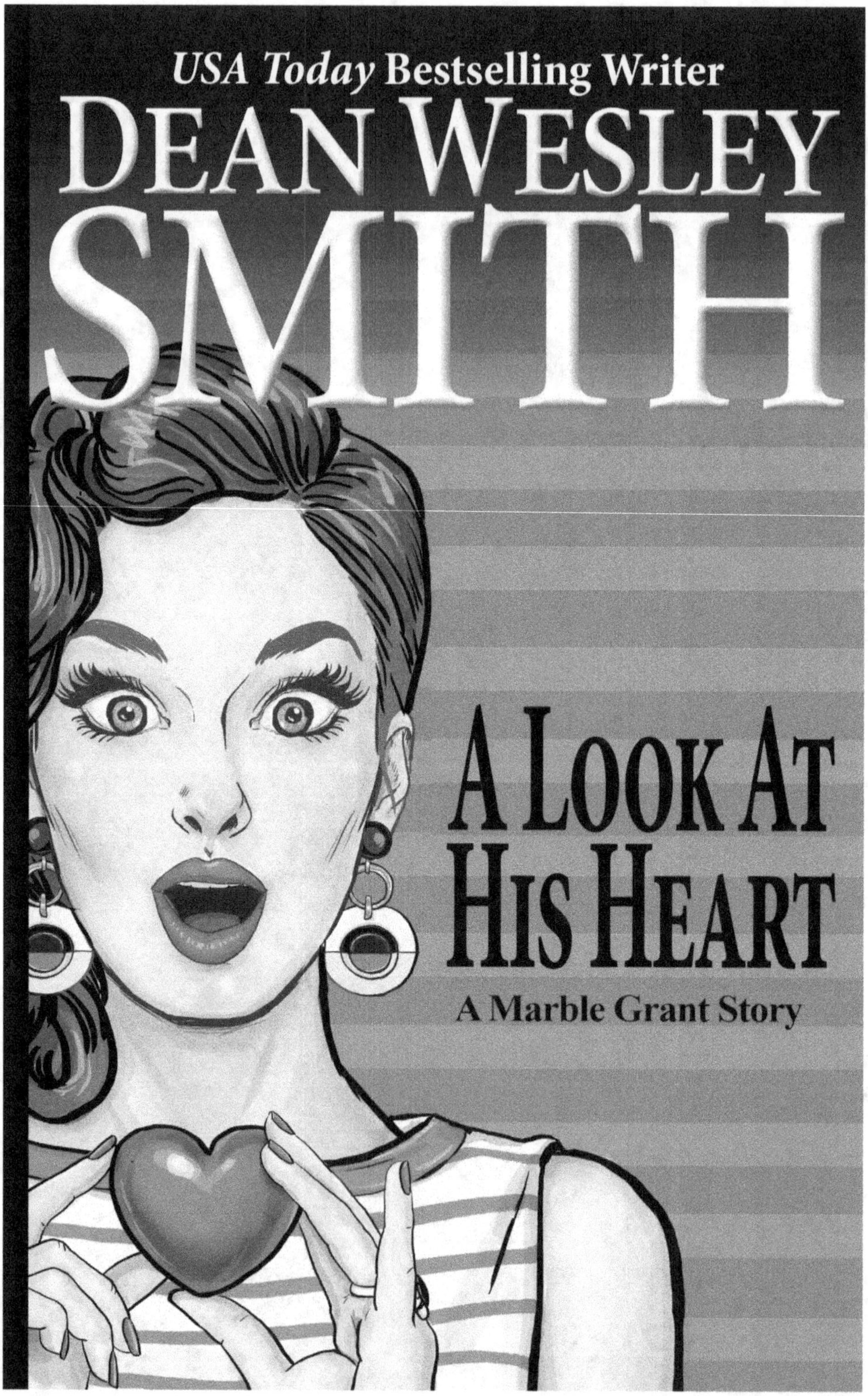
USA Today Bestselling Writer
DEAN WESLEY
SMITH
A LOOK AT
HIS HEART
A Marble Grant Story

Marble Grant and her partner, Sim, discover a handsome and new superhero about to die suddenly of a heart attack.

Canyon Stevens looks completely healthy and right out of a magazine ad.

Can they save him?

Another Marble Grant story with heart, in more ways than one.

A LOOK AT HIS HEART
A Marble Grant Story

ONE

SIM AND I called Wednesday "Heart Day."

After about three months of being a ghost agent team, tasked to help as many people as we could with just about everything, we had decided to make one day a focus on heart attacks.

Wednesday.

Sim and I both loved Wednesdays. Well, actually, we both loved just about any day since we had died, but for some reason, because we had given Wednesday a name, it had become sort of special.

Last night I had tinted my long hair a slightly different color blue for the day and Sim had done her toenails in bright blue. She even let me blow on her toenails to help them dry, which had sent shivers down her back followed by a fit of giggling when I wouldn't stop blowing and a quick trip to our wonderful large bed for far more than just giggling.

One thing I could say about sex while dead. It was a whole lot better than when I was alive, and I thought it pretty good back then. It also might be better because I was head-over-tennis-shoes in love with my beautiful and smart partner and her wonderful trim body.

We had decided last night to start off this Wednesday out on the Strip in front of the MGM Grand Hotel. Now we were not early risers, by any standard, and by the time we had some late breakfast in the Golden Nugget Buffet, it was just before noon.

I had on my normal outfit of jeans, tennis shoes, and a silk blouse. Today, because it was supposed to be a hot fall afternoon, I decided to not wear a bra, which gave Sim a look at my nipples through my blouse anytime she wanted.

I had my off-blue long hair pulled back and wore large dangling earrings.

Sim dressed exactly the same except she had on a bra and had her blonde hair pulled back and up on the back of her head to keep her neck cool. And she had only stud earrings.

Ghost agents felt heat and cold just like anyone did. Maybe even a little more intensely since food tasted more intense and sex felt more intense. Seemed like being a ghost just heightened every sensation.

When we arrived on the hot, wide sidewalk on the Strip, both carrying tall water bottles, it was already full of tourists, most walking slowly in the already warm desert air.

The point of our Heart Day was to find people who were on the verge of having a heart attack and get them help in the local hospital. One of the ghosts who had trained us, Jewel, had been a medical doctor when alive. She had shown us how to go into a person and look for exact signs of a coming heart attack.

Sometimes, if the heart attack was only a distant threat, we planted thoughts in the person's head to get checked up when they got home. But at times, with that kind of focus on looking for one thing, we had actually found a few over the last couple of months we literarily had to rush to a hospital. More than likely we had saved their lives and that felt great, to be honest.

"So where do we start today?" Sim asked, looking at the people passing by.

As Jewel had told us, it was impossible to tell a possible heart attack candidate from the physical appearance alone. Extreme weight, difficulty breathing often meant problems with many other things such as diabetes and cancers. If too many things were wrong like that, Sim and I had decided to just plant suggestions to eat less, exercise more, and get to a doctor as soon as they got home.

Jewel had shown us how to make that suggestion like a nasty itch that needed to be scratched more and more the longer the person waited.

I had lost count of how many heavy people I had seen who were not going to a doctor and who I put that itch need in their minds. I just hoped Jewel was right and it worked. She said it did.

At that moment, I spotted a really handsome man in his mid-thirties, with dark hair, intense dark eyes, and an expensive suit walking toward us. He had no tie on under the suit jacket and his shirt was open two buttons.

He made the day instantly hotter.

The guy walked like he owned the world and was paying no attention to his surroundings or the tourists, so more than likely he was a local.

"You looking at what I am looking at?" Sim asked.

"Trying not to melt," I said.

She laughed and said, "What do you say we climb inside for a ride to cool down."

I just laughed with her, fairly convinced that climbing inside this guy wasn't going to do anything to cool either of us down. It was as if he had walked off the pages of *GQ Magazine*.

As he strode past, both Sim and I melted inside the handsome man.

And then we both started laughing. Not only was he handsome on the outside, this guy was like the perfect man and a superhero to boot.

His name, and I do not kid, was Canyon Stevens.

He was a superhero in the area of sales and business and worked as a high-paying manager of sales of one of the major casino chains. He had been a superhero for only about fifteen years and still didn't have a lot of his powers.

He wasn't even that sure of the ones he did have. They just seemed like normal stuff to him.

I had never heard of the God of Sales that he worked for in the superhero world. There was a lot I didn't know about superheroes and gods and who even ran all us ghost agents.

Canyon loved women, but at the moment he had no girlfriend or wife because he was too busy funding and helping three different start-up businesses around town as well as do his own job. His start-ups helped get jobs for those in need and helped train others in new tech work.

Could this guy get any better?

He lived alone in a nice condo just off the Strip and kept it clean. He had no real vices other than he liked to drink a little too much at times.

I liked to drink like that as well. So did Sim. Even as ghosts we had been known to toss back a few too many.

And that was his only vice.

"This is what our minds would have looked like to a ghost coming in," Sim said.

"Squeaky clean do-gooders," I said.

"Overachievers," Sim said.

"Yeah, that too," I said, laughing.

Canyon had turned and was heading up the sidewalk toward the MGM Hotel lobby. He had a business meeting in an expensive restaurant there, but he stopped suddenly and looked around as if someone was following him.

"Oh, oh," I said. "He senses us."

"Wow," Sim said. "He's pretty good."

At that we both shut up and after a second Canyon shook his head, wondering what he had heard, and headed into the front lobby of the hotel.

The high-ceilinged place was noisy and had a good hundred people milling around. Huge marble pillars separated the area with people's luggage stacked against the pillars in places.

Patty Ledgerwood, aka Front Desk Girl, was standing behind the long wooden check-in desk of the MGM Grand registration. She looked up, beamed, and waved at Canyon, who waved back as he headed across the lobby.

He knew her and was happy to see her. He did not know she was Poker Boy's girlfriend, just that she was a superhero and very nice. But he wasn't attracted to her. He liked his women more like what Sim and I looked like. Tallish, thin, long hair, and a love of sex.

Damn, too bad he was alive and we were dead. Sim and I could have had a blast with him.

"Well, we probably had better drop off this joyride and get to work," Sim said.

"We haven't checked his heart yet," I said, not really wanting to leave Canyon just yet. It wasn't often we got to ride along in a mind that was so clear and without issues.

"Good point," Sim said, laughing.

Again Canyon stopped and looked around.

Sim and I did what Jewel had taught us to do and focused in on the pumping heart of Canyon. It looked fine, no sign at all of heart problems that I could see.

"What the hell is that?" Sim asked.

I looked closer and saw what she was looking at.

A bubble of some sort, or a growth, seemed to have expanded off the back of Canyon's heart. It did not look healthy in any fashion.

In fact, it looked like it might explode with any heartbeat.

Shit, just shit.

TWO

CANYON WAS WAITING with a few tourists now to get on an elevator to take him to the restaurant for his meeting. He knew he was hearing voices, but he couldn't figure out from where.

Or why.

It didn't have him panicked, just puzzled.

The man was about as calm as they came.

"Get Jewel," I said to Sim. "I'll stop him from getting on this elevator."

"Why stop me?" Canyon said out loud.

Sim vanished and I felt stunned that Canyon could hear me that clearly.

A couple of the tourists just looked at him and Canyon covered nicely by pointing at his ear as if talking on a phone they couldn't see.

"Just move away from the elevator and hold on," I said as clear as I could to Canyon. "My name is Marble Grant and I'm a ghost agent who used to be a superhero like you."

Canyon just shook his head, but moved away from the elevator and out of the traffic pattern.

A moment later Jewel appeared and she and Sim joined me inside of Canyon.

"He can hear us clearly," I said to them.

"Yes, I can," he said out loud.

"Back right there," Sim said to Jewel.

Jewel took one look at the problem and said simply, "Shit."

"Well, that doesn't sound promising," Canyon said, "for whatever you are doing."

"Hang tight," I said to Canyon.

We all stepped outside of Canyon and stood beside him.

Jewel was about our height and dressed almost identically as Sim and I. And she looked as worried as I had ever seen her look.

"He needs a hospital right now and emergency surgery," Jewel said. "I doubt he's going to make it through the day or even to the hospital."

"You're kidding me?" Sim asked, looking over at the handsome and healthy superhero standing beside them looking puzzled.

Even puzzled, Canyon's square jaw and dark, intense eyes made him drop-dead handsome. But it seemed that Mr. Perfect wasn't so perfect after all.

And if we didn't do something quick, dropping dead would be exactly what Mr.

Perfect would be doing. I trusted Jewel completely on that diagnosis.

"He can't jump and we can't jump him," Sim said.

I knew what we need to do. "He needs to get to Patty and she can jump him to the hospital. She's at the front desk right now."

Jewel nodded. "Marble, you get him to Patty. Sim, you come with me and we'll get the hospital staff prepared that he is coming and what to look for."

"I'll shout when Patty and I have him ready to jump," I said.

"I'll find a safe place to jump him in the hospital," Sim said.

They both vanished and I stepped back into Canyon's body.

"I'm back," I said as clearly as I could. "You need to go talk with Patty at the front desk right now."

"Why?" he asked.

"I can make you do it," I said. "But I don't want to. More than enough time for answers on the way. Just get going."

He seemed annoyed, but he turned and headed back toward the lobby.

I decided to not sugarcoat the facts. He seemed like the type that could handle bad news.

"You have on your heart what looks like a large bubble that is about to break," I said. "Two other ghost agents are at the hospital right now getting them ready for you, but we need Patty to jump you there. We do not believe you would survive the cab ride."

I was impressed. He heard every word I said and only panicked a little.

I think if I had a voice in my head telling me I was on the verge of dying, I might be screaming and running in circles with my hands over my head shouting that the body snatchers were invading.

I hoped I wouldn't do that, but fairly certain I would have.

Canyon panicked only a little and his heart rate went up, which scared me more than it did him, I'm sure.

"How did you figure this out?" he asked out loud.

"Accident," I said. "We'll explain after we get this fixed. Right now I have to leave you to talk with Patty. Just stand and smile at her."

He stopped in front of the long check-in desk of the hotel as I left his body.

Patty was surprised to see me appear like that suddenly out of the side of Canyon.

I walked through the desk and got close to her as she waited on a live person with two kids trying to check in.

"Canyon there has a bubble about to explode on his heart," I said. "Going to kill him at any moment. Jewel and Sim are at the hospital getting doctors ready. Can you jump him to Sim?"

USA *Today* Bestselling Writer

DEAN WESLEY SMITH

I'M HER DEAD HUSBAND

Now Available
from all your favorite booksellers.

Patty pretended to cover her ear as if talking on a headpiece, then said, "Yes, I can do that. In the hall to the right behind the counter."

I went back to Canyon and slipped back inside him, something I had to admit I was enjoying. And would enjoy as long as he kept living.

"We go through the door in the counter to the right and into the hallway beyond," I told him.

He looked at Patty and she nodded as she got another person to take over what she was doing for the couple.

"She can see you?"

"If I'm outside of you," I said, "yes she can."

Without me giving much direction, he got buzzed through the door in the counter and with Patty at his side the three of us went down the hallway.

"Sim, we're coming," I said out loud to my partner.

"I'm in a no-person, no-camera area," I heard Sim's voice say. "I'll jump back and direct Patty."

An instant later Sim appeared next to Patty.

"Can I give you where to jump to?" Sim asked her.

"Please," Patty said.

I stayed inside Canyon and watched as Sim touched Patty's arm.

Patty nodded and a moment later all of us were in a corridor in the hospital.

"Thanks, Patty," Sim said.

"Good luck," Patty said to Canyon. "You are in the best hands possible."

With that she jumped back to work.

Canyon was now feeling very worried, but focused on moving forward. He really was a superhero considering that at this very moment he was supposed to be eating lunch with a client.

Five very short minutes later I was standing beside Sim out of Canyon after giving him some help calming down and reminding him to call his lunch date and apologize.

Jewel was inside one of the heart surgeons, doing quick tests on Canyon and getting emergency images of Canyon's heart, telling the woman where to look and what to look for.

Less than one hour later they wheeled Canyon into surgery.

Not a damn thing we could do at that point but wait.

Jewel stayed in the doctor's head for the surgery and we jumped to the MGM Grand to tell Patty that Canyon was in surgery.

Then we jumped back to our condo to get lunch and wait for news.

I hate waiting.

Sim seemed to hate it as much as I did.

THREE

JUST OVER TWO hours after they wheeled Canyon into the operating room, Jewel called us and we jumped back to her side in the hospital.

We were standing in a recovery room and Canyon was in a bed covered with a sheet and more tubes and tape than I could imagine having stuck in and on one human body. All around him machines were working, showing stuff I had no clue as to meaning.

Two nurses hovered over him.

All I knew was that Jewel was smiling.

"You two saved his life," she said. "That was a hereditary problem that if you hadn't caught would have burst and killed him almost instantly at any point."

Heart Day just got better.

I hugged Sim and she hugged me back.

"He's going to need a bunch of care once he gets out of here," Jewel said. "You two up for the task, since he has no family?"

I was shocked. "Us?"

"Never imagined myself as Nancy Nurse," Sim said, glancing at the covered body of Canyon.

"I can find you the costume I am sure," I said. "It would be sexy on you."

Jewel and Sim both laughed and Sim hugged me again.

"I think I can get Laverne to allow him to see us," Jewel said. "I'll help you and check in on him as well as his human doctors will."

"We do have a spare bedroom," I said, smiling at my partner.

"I am sure Patty can get Poker Boy to put a hospital bed in there for a short time," Jewel said.

"How long are we talking?" Sim asked a moment before I could.

Jewel shrugged. "He will be out of here in about six days from the looks of how healthy he is other than that bubble. He will need about three weeks, maybe a month of watching and care before he should go back to living alone."

"We would need a live person to cook some meals," I said.

"I have a hunch that Madge on Poker Boy's team might be willing to help with that," Jewel said, "and jump the meals to your place until he can cook for himself."

I looked into the wonderful blue eyes of my partner and smiled. "You up for it?"

She nodded. "Something new, and he is damn nice to look at, you have to admit."

"He is at that," I said. "Especially after he gets healthy again."

So six days later, with Jewel watching carefully, we helped Poker Boy and Patty and Madge get Canyon into our apartment.

It turned out that except for a few issues in the first few days, Canyon was a perfect patient. He did as instructed and let the two of us boss him around.

For the first week, either Sim or I were always there with him. But after that we went back to pretty much our normal routine. And it was on the Wednesday morning, three weeks after we saved Canyon's life, that I went a little too much back to our old routine.

My habit in the morning, before Canyon moved in, was to crawl out of bed stark naked, go into the kitchen where Sim had a cup of coffee waiting for me, take the coffee, and go back to the bathroom and shower.

As I reached the kitchen, still mostly sound asleep, I heard a wolf whistle from Sim, who was sitting at the kitchen table.

And beside her was a very healthy-looking Canyon, smiling.

"Don't get any ideas, mister," I said to his smile. "You ain't healthy enough to handle this yet."

With that, I toasted them with my coffee mug and turned and headed for the bathroom as they both laughed.

And from that moment on the three of us were fine.

We became not only friends, but roommates.

Canyon started cooking and we learned that not only was he good for the eye, he knew how to cook some amazing meals. He said he had almost stopped cooking because he hated cooking only for himself. He loved cooking for us because he only made enough for just himself, but all three of us could eat.

And as he got feeling better, his true sense of humor and dry wit came out. And his fantastic intelligence. He could see things with people that both Sim and I would miss.

When he left, I was not only going to miss him as a friend, I was going to miss his sense of humor, his calmness, his incredible good looks, and his fantastic cooking.

When Jewel finally gave Canyon the all-clear to go back to his condo after three weeks, both Sim and I just sort of moped around.

I mean I hadn't been that depressed in a long time, and Sim said she felt the same way.

We talked about drinking, but that felt like a little too much work.

Our wonderful condo now felt empty.

So we talked about it and we both decided that Canyon, if he wanted, could be part of our team, move back in, and the three of us do what we could to help people.

The idea made us both happy again. But I was really worried that he would turn us down.

After all, he had lived with two mostly crazy ghost women for three weeks.

So instead of worrying about it all night, we went to his place and actually rang his doorbell, something that took both of us to do, and a lot of willpower. We were still not that good at touching and moving real things.

Canyon was surprised to see us standing there in the hall looking worried.

But his smile was genuine.

So he asked us in and we just stood there inside his condo door and blurted out what we were thinking like two schoolgirls afraid we would get turned down.

And as we talked, Canyon's grin got bigger.

"Two new superhero ghost agents and a new superhero business guy teaming up?" he asked.

I nodded. "Pretty much."

"Strangest team in all the land, that would be for sure," Sim said.

"Who knows what we could accomplish," he said, smiling.

"Who knows what could go wrong," Sim said, laughing.

I knew right then that we had him.

"If you say yes," I said, "would you agree to cook at times?"

He laughed and said simply, "I would love to."

"And wear an apron without pants?" Sim asked.

He smiled and looked at Sim, then at me. "Maybe."

"Damn," I said, grasping my chest, "now I'm having a heart attack."

They both laughed.

And with that he got us all drinks and we toasted the formation of our new team.

And the fun we were going to have.

Oh, boy were we going to have fun.

❤

Now Available
from all your favorite booksellers.

Can't Get Enough of Poker Boy?
These stories and more are
available at your favorite booksellers.

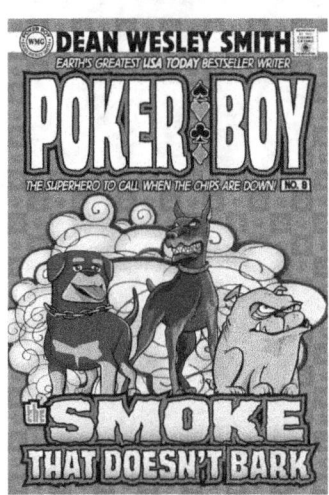

USA *Today* Bestselling Writer

DEAN WESLEY SMITH

WINGS OUT
A Bryant Street Story

Rolanda Campbell finds herself living a life she never could have imagined.

A prison life on a simple suburban street called Bryant Street.

She knew she bore the responsibility for the horrid life.

So finally she took the responsibility for leaving as well. And never once looked back at Bryant Street.

WINGS OUT
A Bryant Street Story

THIS WOULD BE the last time.

Rolanda Campbell stretched and stood from her recliner, looking around the modern living room, dark because of the blinds being pulled against the sun.

A long, uncomfortable couch he had picked out to match an even more uncomfortable love seat filled one wall in front of the window, its off-yellow color looking like dried puke in the wrong light.

The fake-stone fireplace had never been used, of course. Too dirty.

Her tan recliner facing the large screen television mounted over the fireplace matched his, and with two pillows she had managed to make it comfortable for her thin, five-five frame.

Out of habit she fluffed the two pillows and put them back exactly where they belonged on the couch.

Then, just for the hell of it, she tossed the pillows into the middle of the living room floor. That would drive the bastard nuts.

This morning would be the last time she would ever watch those morning shows and deal with the pressure of trying to be perfect for a man who didn't know perfect, but believed he did.

Every morning now for three years, since their honeymoon, Rolanda had gotten out of bed ahead of her husband, showered, dressed as if she was going to a business meeting in expensive pant-suits, put on makeup as he expected her to do, and made him breakfast.

The exact same breakfast. Same two eggs over easy, same white toast with strawberry jam, same slice of ham. Heaven help her if she overcooked his eggs.

She would have been so much more comfortable in jeans and tennis shoes and a cotton blouse, but he wanted her to look her best for him when he left for work. She had caved in to that demand, just as he had worn her down and forced her into this life in the first place.

Then she ate lightly with him at the breakfast table because he didn't want her to get fat.

Then as she did the dishes, he read his morning journals on his iPad without saying a word, then put it in his briefcase, kissed her on the cheek, thanked her for breakfast, and left for work.

All very civil and cold.

Dead cold.

Rolanda's job was to keep the house spotless and have dinner ready for him when he got home. Which she had done for three long, stupid years.

Then they watched a prescribed amount of television together, always what he wanted to watch, then went to bed at the exact same time every night.

Sex had long become a thing of the past for them.

What they were living was his sick image of a perfect marriage.

Perfect in his mind, not in hers.

She had a master's in interior design and had married him right out of school, thinking they would be a perfect match.

Instead she had made herself in three short years into a prisoner to a man she now detested.

One year ago, she had finally hit her limit and tried to talk with him about what she wasn't happy about. At that point she still thought the marriage might be saved.

She really was that stupid.

It was a first marriage and she had no other family. She had no way of knowing otherwise.

He would have none of her problems. They were married, she was his wife, she would not leave him, she would do as he asked.

End of discussion.

Things went right back to the way they had been as if nothing had happened.

To her own disgust at herself, she had backed down.

And shut up.

It wasn't as if he hit her. He never had.

She doubted he ever would.

But she had become deathly afraid of him anyway. And she had no idea why.

She desperately needed to understand why in the very near future. But for now, she had things to do today, not normal things, very different things.

It was time she took her life back.

Six months ago she had saved enough from the grocery money he allowed her to hire a private detective to see what the bastard husband did every day. It took her a few thousand, but she finally discovered bastard husband went to work as an accountant as he said he did, but was sleeping with a waitress from a restaurant three lunches a day.

If she confronted him with the fact, he would either deny it or say it was his right as a man to do just that. After all, didn't he provide the perfect home for her and pay all the bills?

So Rolanda hadn't said a word, just kept doing her "job" as he expected.

But it was with that discovery she had decided to finally take back her pride and finish this entire thing.

She clicked off the morning shows and acting as calm as the bastard always did, she moved to the house computer in an alcove off the dining room. She had hired help from a local computer store to come and undo all the locks and safety features the bastard husband had put on the home computer to keep her contained.

Using the files the detective had given her, and accounts she had opened under her maiden name in three banks, she moved all of their money to her accounts.

It was a lot more money than she had expected because until that moment she had never dared check the accounts. But honestly she didn't care. She left him none of it.

Not one penny.

She called the attorney she had hired a few months before and said to serve the divorce papers on the bastard.

The woman attorney, named Steph, said, "With pleasure."

The attorney had pictures of Rolanda's bastard husband with the waitress, so no divorce would be contested. Not even with an ego like the bastard husband had. He didn't dare show that side of himself in public. That would shatter the illusion of perfection he worked too hard to maintain.

And that Rolanda had gone along with.

Steph had asked Rolanda if she wanted the house, since she could get it in the divorce, but all that had done was make her shudder. She just wanted out.

With that all done, she then called her husband's boss, a man by the name of Stratton.

She knew her husband would be in the hotel room with the waitress at that point.

She asked if he was alone and they could talk.

Stratton said he was.

She then told him that she was divorcing her husband for infidelity, but today when she got access to their accounts, she realized he had a lot more money than should be there and there was evidence her husband had been moving some money into other accounts she couldn't access.

"Are you being vindictive?" Stratton asked, his voice cold.

"No," she said, lying through her teeth. "I could be, but I am far past that, to be honest. I am leaving my husband because he has been screwing a waitress. I am just trying to do you a service is all and tell you what I found today when I got my money from his accounts. You might want to investigate quietly. The private detective I hired thinks he saw some pretty fishy things as well. But that is up to you. It is your business. I honestly don't care."

With that she hung up, smiling.

Her husband's perfect life was just going to be messed up something awful today.

She knew, without a doubt or excuse, that she had been at fault for letting him do this to her. She flat knew that. She had only wanted her marriage to work and at first she had been happy to go along.

Not anymore.

Once she got settled in her new life and found a job in her profession, the first thing she would do would be to find a counselor and figure out why she had allowed herself to get into this situation.

And stay in it for so long.

She had a hunch it was because of the fear of suddenly being alone in the large world and her perfect husband gave her the foundation she had needed for a short time.

But she had allowed it to go on for three years.

She knew she never would again.

She moved into their bedroom, the last time she would ever be in that room, and took out the two packed suitcases from the back of the closet, then changed into jeans, tennis shoes, and a cotton blouse. She left all the expensive pantsuits he had wanted her to wear hanging in the closet.

His dozen suits, all matching dark blue, hung in rows on his side of the closet, everything in its perfect place, his dark shoes lined up below the suits.

She went to the bathroom and got a small bottle of acid from under the sink where she had hidden it. It was for burning off corns, but it put really nice holes in fabric.

She carefully put one drop of acid on each suit coat, right behind the shoulder where it would be clear to anyone and impossible to fix, one drop of acid on the toe of each shoe, and one drop of acid on the crotch of each of his slacks.

Then she sprinkled the rest of the acid on his perfectly folded underwear in his drawer. She had folded them all.

His perfect look was soon going to have some holes in it.

That made her laugh for the first time in longer than she could remember.

The sound seemed very strange in that bedroom.

She glanced at the clock.

Mr. Perfect Husband would now be halfway done with his mistress. The papers would be served to him when they came walking out in about fifteen minutes. Even in an affair, the bastard was punctual and predictable and boring.

But right now, Rolanda needed to vanish.

She needed to move on with her life, but just for fun, she had one more little annoyance to toss at Mr. Perfect.

One more stab into whatever tiny little heart the man had. If she could get through his ego to even reach his heart.

She left her driver's license with her married name on the dresser along with the one credit card he allowed her for groceries and to buy clothes. She already had a new credit card and a new driver's license under her maiden name.

She put her phone beside the license. She already had a new phone as well.

And under that she pulled out of her second drawer a picture of Mr. Perfect and the waitress. Both were naked. The shot had been taken with a long-range camera by the detective. The lawyer had a copy of that photo and some other choice ones as well.

Under the picture Rolanda had a note that said, "If you want your wife to be perfect, you must also be perfect. Just a suggestion for your next wife."

Then she pulled out her new phone and called for a ride from the private detective she had hired. He was standing by in a café four blocks away just in case she ran into trouble today.

The detective was a great guy. Handsome, clearly talented, and he liked her. Given a little time, who knew where that would lead.

But first she needed the time to be alone, to be in her own place, to live the way she wanted to live.

She needed to fly on her own for a while.

And not be perfect.

With two suitcases in hand, she walked to the front door and looked back at the home she had cleaned continuously for three straight years.

She glanced out the window. Her detective friend wasn't here yet, so maybe just one or two more little things to stab at Mr. Perfect just a little more.

She went to the closet and took out the vacuum cleaner and plugged it in, then with the cord spread along the ground and around a couple chairs, she left the vacuum in the hallway right in front of the front door.

She turned on the television, fairly loud, and tossed the remotes into the garbage can under the sink, under the morning's waste where he would never look for them.

She left the dishwasher door standing open.

And then she opened all the blinds in the living room, letting in the sunshine, something he never allowed for fear it would fade the furniture.

There was now light where there had been darkness.

As she looked out the window, the private detective pulled up.

She grabbed her two suitcases and, skipping like a college girl, headed down the front sidewalk, leaving the front door wide open.

She never looked back at the prison she had made for herself.

She had finally escaped.

She was now free. Free to fly.

And she planned on doing a lot of flying.

~

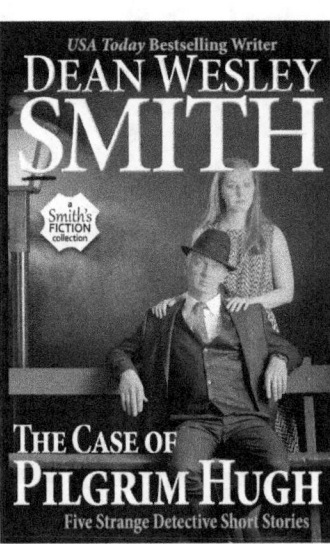

Now Available!
Five-Story Collections in Some of Dean Wesley Smith's Most Popular Series. Find them at your favorite booksellers!

USA TODAY BESTSELLING AUTHOR

DEAN WESLEY SMITH

HEINLEIN'S RULES

FIVE SIMPLE BUSINESS RULES FOR WRITING

A WMG WRITER'S GUIDE

With more than a hundred published novels and more than seventeen million copies of his books in print, USA Today *bestselling author Dean Wesley Smith follows five simple business rules for writing fiction. And now, he shares how those rules helped shape his successful career.*

In this WMG Writer's Guide, Dean takes you step-by-step through Heinlein's Rules and shows how following those rules can change your writing—and career—for the better.

Simple rules, yet deceptively hard to follow. Do you have the courage to take a hard look at your writing process and follow Heinlein's Rules? Dean shows you how.

HEINLEIN'S RULES
Five Simple Business Rules for Writing
A WMG Writer's Guide

For all the writers who dare to follow these business rules. Have fun.

INTRODUCTION

IN ALMOST 150 published novels (over one hundred with traditional publishers), I have always followed Heinlein's Business Rules. And in hundreds and hundreds of short stories, I have followed the five rules as well.

For well over thirty years now, actually, I have done my best to stay on Heinlein's Rules. I must admit, I slipped at times, but I'll explain why later on in the book. And how I climbed back on.

So how did I get to these rules? A little about my personal story first.

I started writing at the age of 24 in 1974.

I had hated writing up until that point, but I had to take some English credits to get my degree in architecture, so I took a poetry class for non-majors.

My poems were pretty much hated and the professor called them "commercial." At that point, I had no idea what she was talking about, but it sounded insulting and I was getting a "C" in the class.

Commercial seemed very, very bad.

Then, as an assignment, she had her entire class mail a poem to a major national college poetry competition. One of my "commercial" poems won second place and paid me one hundred bucks. The professor had never had a student even get into the book, let alone win.

And I had just made more money than she had total with all of her poetry sales.

Oh, oh... To say I was not popular in the English Department would be an understatement.

But I found writing poems fun and started mailing them out and selling them to top literary journals around the

More WMG Writer's Guides
from all your favorite booksellers
in trade paper and electronic editions.

country. Great fun. Seemed major literary magazines liked commercial.

Sold around fifty or so in one year.

And along the way, I thought it would be a lark to write a short story.

So on my trusty electric typewriter, I banged out a 1,000-word story, and didn't rewrite it, just sent it to a horror semi-pro magazine.

They bought it.

I did it again.

They bought the second one.

Spring of 1975 was when things went really wrong. I figured since I was having fun with writing stories, I should learn more about how to write stories, even though I had sold my first two.

So down I went into the myths of writing. (Add bubbling sounds of a person going underwater for the last time.)

I heard I needed to rewrite at least three or four times, so I did, even though I hated to type.

I heard I had to write slow to make it good, so I did, producing exactly two short stories a year for the next seven years.

And every story I thought was gold, a perfect masterpiece of fine art.

All of them were form rejected. And I made it worse by sending each story out only once or twice.

I was convinced the editors were too stupid to see my brilliance.

The two stories I had not touched or rewritten and wrote fast had sold, but the reality was I was too stupid to understand that. I believed in the myths and would defend them, by golly.

But after seven years, by the fall of 1981, I was very, very discouraged. I started looking around at how the writers I admired did what they did.

Bradbury, Silverberg, Ellison all wrote fast, one draft, and never rewrote past a few minor corrections. And I studied the old pulp writers I admired. Same thing. And I dug through the stories of the literary writers like Hemingway and others. Same thing.

Then by chance, I ran across an edition of *Of Worlds Beyond: The Science of Science Fiction Writing.*

Edited by Lloyd Arthur Eshbach, published in 1947, the book had articles in it by John Taine, Jack Williamson, A.E. van Vogt, L. Sprague de Camp, E. E. "Doc" Smith, John W. Campbell, Jr., and Robert A. Heinlein.

All of the articles are forgettable, sadly, including Heinlein's article, except for the last four paragraphs.

He starts the last four paragraphs with this:

"I'm told that these articles are supposed to be some use to the reader. I have a guilty feeling that all of the above may have been more for my amusement than for your edification. Therefore I shall chuck in as a bonus a group of practical, tested rules, which, if followed meticulously, will prove rewarding to any writer."

Then in one more paragraph he lists his "business habits."

1. You must write.

2. You must finish what you start.

3. You must refrain from rewriting except to editorial order.

4. You must put it on the market.

5. You must keep it on the market until sold.

Then Heinlein said this:

"The above five rules really have more to do with how to write speculative fiction than anything said above them. But they are amazingly hard to follow— which is why there are so few professional writers and so many aspirants, *and which is why I am not afraid to give away the racket! ..."*

I finally understood completely what I had been doing wrong for seven long years. And why my first two stories had sold.

Duh.

So on January 1st, 1982, I made a resolution to write a story per week, following Heinlein's Rules, and mail the story and keep it in the mail.

I wrote 44 stories that first year and started selling regularly in early 1983 and have never looked back.

And stayed focused on those five rules to this day.

Why So Difficult?

The reason these rules are so hard is that they fly into the face, solidly, of what every English teacher on the planet teaches. And has taught from even before Heinlein wrote the rules down.

But remember, English teachers are there to do the almost impossible job of helping students gather knowledge about the language.

They are not there to help a student become a professional fiction writer.

So these simple five business rules smash right into all that learning and teaching we all had as regular English students.

And with the modern world of computers, rewriting is easy, much easier, let me tell you, than it was on a typewriter. So not doing it is even more difficult.

Also, these five rules smash into so many writing myths, it will take most of this book to just detail out how each rule will cause many people to be uncomfortable.

Or even angry.

If one of these rules makes you angry, you need to check in with yourself. Your critical voice is really, really having issues and trying to stop you.

So over the course of this book, I'm going to work through each of the five rules, explaining why the rule is important to becoming a professional fiction writer, how missing a rule stops millions of writers, and how to use the rule in this modern world to access your creative voice and bring fun into your fiction writing.

One note: This is a book about fiction writing. This book is designed to help you on the road to being a professional fiction writer. This does not apply to nonfiction writers or writers of critical essays and the like.

Heinlein was talking about fiction writing. Please keep that clearly in mind.

In 1947, Robert A. Heinlein "...gave away the racket!"

But also, as he said, almost no one can follow these five business rules.

I hope to help you become one of the few who can.

And thus have a long fiction-writing career and fun with your writing.

CHAPTER ONE

For lack of a better way of putting it, Heinlein's Rules allow you to get to the fun of being a writer.

They also help us all remember we are entertainers.

About a decade or so ago, I was asked by a professor of English at the University of Oregon to come talk to one of his advanced creative writing classes about the reality of being a full-time fiction writer.

I had a hunch I was going to not do nice things to their brains. And I looked on that possibility as my sacred job description.

But it turned out I was the one shocked. Before I even had a chance to start to tell them about the fun of writing, about making a living, about writing *Star Trek* or *Men in Black*, one of the students said basically, Mr. Smith, did you know you put such-and-such theme in your story?

I could barely remember the story he was asking about, and I had zero idea that theme was even in there. I know for a fact I didn't layer that in on purpose.

As I sort of sat there facing them, three of them got into an argument about what one of my stories really meant. The poor professor had to stop them to let me talk.

I had no clue any of the stuff they were talking about was even in the story. Clearly it was, but their attitude about it and how important that was to them shocked me down to my little toes, let me tell you.

I'm an entertainer.

It never occurs to me to add that literary stuff in purposely. But clearly it is there.

Kris had a similar experience back in the Midwest with a college class.

And then another time I got this same lesson in a different way. About twenty years ago, Kris and I were walking along and I asked her which magazine she thought a story I had finished the night before should go. She suggested a market and then said, "It's one of your wonderful prison stories."

"I don't write prison stories," I said.

I think it took her ten minutes to stop laughing.

It seems, after she explained it to me, that all of my stories, in one fashion or another, are about real people being trapped in some form or another.

Could have fooled me.

I just write to entertain myself.

I guess I have some issues that are deep-seated (or deep-seeded, which makes more sense in this case) about being trapped.

But it clearly seems that when I get out of my own way with my writing, my subconscious layers in all sorts of deep and meaningful stuff I don't even think about.

Go figure.

And, of course, that's how it has always been with writers.

We write to entertain. It is up to others to figure out what we wrote.

And Heinlein's five business rules help us get to the point where we are just writing and letting the art stuff happen.

Would I have ever gotten to that point of putting that cool stuff (without knowing) in my stories without Heinlein's Rules?

Nope.

Would I have made a living with my fiction for the last numbers of decades without Heinlein's Rules?

Nope.

Would I be enjoying writing as much as I do without Heinlein's Rules?

Not a chance.

Here is My Attitude in Clear Form

—I never look back. I am always focused on the story and then the next story.

—Others can look back for me, either as readers or in some university class. I don't care.

—I write to entertain, first myself, then readers. That is my focus.

—I write because it's the most fun I can have at this age. (No jokes, please.)

I think that understanding my attitude will help all readers of this book color how I look at these five simple rules.

One Thing Heinlein's Rules Does Not Talk About

Heinlein's Rules say nothing about typing fast.

They say nothing about speed or anything associated with being prolific.

So many people think they do, but they do not.

For some reason this gets confused and mixed into the rules, but please, if you catch yourself thinking about speed or productivity in association with these five rules, stop and step back.

Heinlein's Rules are business rules.

So with all that said, onward into the rules.

CHAPTER TWO

Rule #1 … You must write.

How simple.

On the surface, this sounds so easy. Of course, just write. Duh.

Well, how about some reality?

Say you have one million people who say they want to be writers, who have a book in them they really want to write, who have a dream about writing stories and maybe getting published.

One million. There are a lot more than that, of course, but for this example that number is round.

My opinion, of that one million, nine hundred thousand will never find the time.

That's just my rough and more-than-likely conservative guess. But it is a guess on my part from decades of watching.

Nine out of ten people can't find the time to write, even though they say they want to.

Or another way to look at this, in my opinion over 90% of all people who say they would like to write, who say they want to write someday, are wiped out by Heinlein's Rule #1.

Yeah, the first rule sounds so, so, so simple, doesn't it?

You must write.

Period.

Yet it is the most deadly of all the rules.

Writer vs. Author

My definition of a writer is a person who writes.

My definition of an author is a person who has written.

Yeah, I agree, sort of a nasty distinction. I have no respect for authors. I have a ton of respect for writers.

(And right there a massive herd of authors just left this book. Ahhh, well, they had promotion to do, after all.)

In this modern world of indie publishing, we see a ton of authors out there pushing their one or two or three books, promoting them to death, annoying their two hundred Twitter followers and their family on Facebook.

Promotion is not writing. That's just being an author.

Writers are people who write.

Also, Heinlein did not say, *You must research.*

Research is not writing.

Also, Heinlein did not say, *You must promote.*

Promotion of your last novel is not writing.

Talking with your friends in a workshop about your future book is not writing.

Outlining your novel is not writing.

And on and on.

Back to *Rule #1: You must write.*

So simple.

So hard for so many.

My friend Kevin J. Anderson sent me a wonderful card when I sold my first novel. I sold my first novel about a year ahead of his first novel sale, yet he clearly understood what was going on better than I did at that point.

The card was priceless, and I still have it.

On the front the card was divided into six panels. Each panel showed this mouse sweating to push this huge elephant up a hill.

And with each panel the elephant got higher on the hill.

I opened the card and there, inside, was the elephant sitting at the top of the hill and the mouse looking down at a herd of elephants in a valley below.

More WMG Writers' Guides
from all your favorite booksellers
in trade paper and electronic editions.

The caption on the card said, "Congratulations! Now, do it again."

Exactly.

Now, almost thirty years later (I sold that first novel in May of 1987) I am still having a great time moving those elephants to the top of the hill, one right after another.

Writers are people who write.

I am a writer.

And thanks to Heinlein's Rules, especially Rule #1, I make my living writing fiction.

And I have since 1987.

CHAPTER THREE

Still working on Rule #1.

Rule #1: You Must Write.

Back in 1982, when I climbed onto my challenge to use Heinlein's Rules and write a story per week and mail each story every week, I had one major issue that I fought.

Fear.

No idea what I was afraid of, but the fear was real.

On December 31st, 1981, my thinking was that every story had to be perfect, had to be worked over and over before I dared send it out. And it had to be written slowly and carefully to be good. I believed everything English teachers taught me.

Hook, line, and sinker.

One day later, January 1st, 1982, I went to Heinlein's Rules, not rewriting, writing a story and just mailing it after fixing typos.

Cold turkey.

So from that moment forward, I thought that every story I sent out was crap. Total crap.

I didn't just think that, I believed it completely.

I had no doubt. None.

I was still in the "must be perfect" mode (kidding myself that I knew what perfect even was, of course).

But I was going to give the Heinlein's Rules challenge a try because so many major writers wrote that way and I had had no luck at all the other way for seven years.

So week after week, I mailed off stories I thought sucked. Oh, I did my best on them, made sure they were as typo-free as possible, but I spent no time on them as I had with my precious two-stories-per-year gems that sat molding in files.

And fairly quickly the form rejections turned to personal letters and then to nice letters from editors. Shock!

Then early in the second year I started selling. I sold to *Writers of the Future, Oui Magazine, Gem Magazine*, and to a Damon Knight edited anthology. (You can still read my story in volume #1 of *Writers of the Future.)*

And the sales kept rolling in.

I still thought every story I wrote was crap.

Every one of them.

But I was starting to catch a clue that if I just let my subconscious tell the story and stay out of its way, my stories were pretty good.

Also, I kept learning and seeking out details of advice that made sense with my new way of approaching things.

What was also happening at writing a story per week was that I was practicing. I wrote more in the first fifteen weeks of 1982 than I did in the previous seven years.

Any wonder my stuff got better?

You Must Write.

I had figured out a way to do that.

Dare to be Bad

One fine day during that first year, I was complaining to the great fantasy writer Nina Kiriki Hoffman about how I felt I was mailing out crap every week. Sure, I was starting to get nice letters from editors, but I still couldn't get past the training of wanting to make every story "perfect."

And I felt like I often wrote stories too quickly, so they couldn't be good.

Yup, even six months or so into the challenge of following Heinlein's Rules, I was still lost in the myths. Completely.

Nina was living above my bookstore and she was doing the same challenge I was. We had bet each other to get a new story per week out.

Now I was in law school, had a job tending bar, and I owned and ran a bookstore. I was married and I had no time to write a story per week, but I was doing it.

Nina was still in college. She had no time either. But she was doing it also.

So in response that day to my complaining about how I felt I was mailing out crap, Nina basically said, "It takes more courage to try something and fail than to not try at all."

We talked about how true that was, and Nina coined the phrase "Dare to be bad."

It takes more courage to write and put the story out than it does to only talk about writing and not do it. You have to dare to fail sometimes.

So I took that saying and stenciled it in big letters and tacked it on the wall over my typewriter in my bookstore.

Dare to be bad.

What that saying did to help me seemed critical in one area. That saying got me past the fear of writing.

Rule #1: You Must Write.

What stops most people isn't lack of time, it's fear.

Committing words to paper means you might have to show them to someone. The words might fail; you might be found wanting.

So it is easier to let the fear stop you before you even get to Rule #1.

Most people who say they would like to write are just too afraid and don't know how to get past the fear.

The "Dare to be Bad" saying helped me jump past the fear.

And what that ultimately did was allow my subconscious to do the work.

My job became, fairly quickly, staying out of the way of my subconscious and just mailing the final product, no matter what my conscious brain thought of it.

That's right. I have trained my critical front brain to just stay out of the way of the storyteller that is my back brain.

Easier said than done, and still a constant fight.

To this day, when I hand a story or a novel to Kris, I believe it is crap. I have learned my critical judgment means nothing when it comes to my own work.

And when Kris hands me something she wrote and says it sucks, I know I am in for a real treat.

Why?

Because if Kris's critical brain is afraid of something she wrote, that means she took chances, went to places she had never been before, took risks with the story or the writing.

And she knows that even if she thinks the story sucks, she needs to release it to someone who has perspective.

Kris won a Hugo Award for her editing, and yet with her own work, she can't judge it.

No writer can.

So does that mean the fear isn't real that we all feel?

Nope. It's a real fear.

Trust me, I feel it with every story or novel I finish.

But the only repercussion on the negative side is that you allow the fear to win. If you release the story, you quickly come to see that the fear is baseless.

Doesn't make it feel any less real, however.

And it is this fear of some made-up repercussion that stops most of the 90% of writers who say they want to write and can't find the time.

Anyone can find the time to write a little every day.

But only about 1 in 10 can figure out a way, as I did, to climb past the fear, or just live with the fear of failure by writing.

It is better to write and fail than not write at all.

Rule #1. You must write.

Dare to be Bad.

You might discover along the way just how good a storyteller your subconscious really is.

I did.

CHAPTER FOUR

Moving now to the second rule.

Rule #2: You Must Finish What You Write.

Say 9 out of 10 people who claim they want to write are wiped out by Rule #1 because they "just can't find the time."

If that is the case, then my guess is that another half of the remaining writers are stopped cold by Rule #2.

Now, I have to be honest, I never had an issue with this rule, so I mostly just ignored it. I always finished what I wrote. Part of that was the early challenge to mail a story per week, but mostly I just hate leaving things unfinished.

So until Kris and I started teaching workshops, I had no idea how really deadly this not-finishing-projects was to many, many writers. I just had no idea, because it is not my problem.

So I talked with a lot of writers over the last fifteen years about various aspects of this problem of not finishing.

And I started watching all the excuses people give for not finishing, and it became clear how really deadly this rule is for many.

At first I thought it was a craft problem writers had. I thought maybe writers didn't understand the ending structure, or how to build to an end, or even how to see an ending.

Sure, there were minor aspects of that, but when that was scraped away, it boiled down to a few common problems I'll detail below.

How It Works

The feeling of this problem goes like this for many:

Step one: Excitement about a story or an idea.

Step two: Excitement carries the writer a distance into the story or novel or an outline.

Step three: Excitement wears off, critical voice plows in, story looks like crap and is too much work to keep going.

Step four: Writer makes up some excuse to stop and go find a project that is exciting again.

Step five: Repeat the first four steps without ever finishing anything.

Outlines do not help this problem.

Finishing has been made into an "important event" and thus almost impossible to actually get to. Like that pot of gold at the end of a rainbow.

As long as you are working on something, you can call yourself a writer. But when you finish, you aren't writing, so it is better to stay a writer and just keep working on it.

You can't fail if you just keep working on a project.

Writers with this problem can't see not finishing as failure.

Two Major Areas

1. Fear

To put it simply, finishing something risks that what you finished will fail.

In my early days, failure was the story not selling to an editor. In this modern world, it can still be that, or it can be that you put it out indie and no one buys it.

If you keep working on something to make it better, rewriting it for the fifth time, reworking that plot you don't think works, and so on and so on, you won't risk the failure of no readers in the end.

To writers with this problem, a story must be some imaginary image of "perfect" before it can be released. And no story ever attains that.

For any of us, actually.

Kris did an entire book on this called *The Pursuit of Perfection*. That book deals with this problem and so much more and is worth your time and money if you have this problem.

Fear of failure is real and if it has become the dominating force in your writing, you need to go get professional help to get past the problem. It is that serious. Not kidding.

Rule #3 coming up also works into this rule.

Finishing a sloppy first draft that you must rewrite is not finishing. Sorry.

As long as you are working on a story in some fashion or another, it is not

More WMG Writer's Guides
**from all your favorite booksellers
in trade paper and electronic editions**.

finished, and thus you don't have to risk the fear of failure.

And a small slice of writers have this issue because of fear of success. Not kidding here either. They don't finish because their ego tells them their work is so wonderful, it will be an instant bestseller, and they don't want to be famous.

I have met a couple of these writers. I managed to not laugh until I walked out of the room.

Also, finishing brings in another fear. Fear of mailing.

I have been an editor off and on for over thirty years. Not once do I remember a story that didn't work. Why?

Because editors don't read stories that don't work.

Duh.

I can't even remember the thousands of stories I have bought at various magazines over the years, let alone any story I didn't read.

Duh.

But yet the fear of mailing to an editor scares some writers beyond words. So they are better off not finishing than to have to face that fear.

And now the fear of learning how to indie publish scares writers, so better to not finish than have to learn all the new stuff.

Fear.

On and on.

Excuse after excuse.

2. Love of a Project

This is also fear-based, but in a different way. It goes like this:

"If I finish this project, what do I do next?"

This boils down to the early fear all writers have of not finding another idea. I do a six-week online workshop called "Ideas to Story" that helps writers fix that issue completely.

And as you write more and more, you quickly come to realize that ideas are everywhere and far too many for you to ever get to.

I used to write ideas down in notebooks because of this fear. But after a few years I stopped because if I couldn't remember the idea in a week, it wouldn't be worth my time to write it.

And now I never even come up with ideas.

I don't. Honest.

I write from triggers, an advanced way of telling stories, granted. But given enough time, every writer can get there.

But I do understand this excuse to not finish. I have a number of worlds I love to play inside. But I write and finish stories and novels inside the worlds. I never just work on one thing for years.

But I have seen more writers than I want to admit that are working on "their novel." When they say that, you know this is their problem and Rule #2 is going to kill them.

Writers like this will finish a draft, maybe, then go into major rewrites, even though they have no idea how to rewrite or how to tell a better story, they still need to stir the words around.

Then they give it to some "editor" that they pay a vast amount of money to (called a scam) and the editor has them work on it some more.

And on and on.

Never finishing.

Sadly, I have never seen a writer find a solution to this. They can't even admit the problem to themselves so they just cycle in the same world, same characters.

These writers will never finish because if they finished, all the people around them who had watched them work on "their novel" for years might actually have a chance to read it.

Far, far too dangerous to allow to happen.

You also see this with most of the sloppily drafted NaNoWriMo novels. They will never be fixed and no one will ever read them because it's too dangerous for the writer to let their supportive family who sacrificed time so they could write see how really bad the book might be.

If Writing Is Not Fun

Writers who can't seem to finish much, if anything, believe in the tortured "artist" myth, that writing must be hard and only years of working in the salt mines can make a novel brilliant.

Nope. That's a myth.

Thankfully.

So two major reasons why this simple Rule #2 stops so many writers.

1. Fear of failure.
2. Fear of moving on to something new.

Notice "fear" is the major word in both.

If a fear of any kind is crippling you and stopping you from finishing a novel or story, don't fight the story through. You won't beat the fear that way.

Step outside of that one novel, that one story, and deal with the fear outside of any one story.

What are you afraid will happen?

And is that worse than never finishing anything?

Heinlein's Rules are so simple. Remember, even he said that.

So let me lay out clearly what he meant with the first two rules in relationship to failure and fear of failure.

Think of the rules this way:

Rule #1...You Must Write. Not writing is failure.

Rule #2...You Must Finish What You Write. Not finishing is failure.

So if you are having fear issues, move the fear over to not writing and not finishing.

Former PGA Golf Professional and USA Today *bestselling writer Dean Wesley Smith walks you step-by-step, club-by-club from your car to the first tee and beyond in a laugh-out-loud style that not only teaches, but entertains.*

A perfect gift for the golfer in your family.

Now Available
from all your favorite booksellers in trade paper and electronic editions.

I can tell you this for a fact: The idea of not writing and not finishing what I write scares hell out of me.

Get help with your fears, move the fear to a fear of not writing.

And move the fear to a fear of not finishing.

Because not writing and not finishing are true failures.

I hate to tell you this folks: Every time you claim you want to write and then don't write or don't finish, everyone around you knows you are failing.

That should scare you more than anything.

CHAPTER FIVE

Moving now to the third rule.

Rule #3: You Must Refrain from Rewriting Unless to Editorial Order.

So, this is the rule that gets all the attention here in the modern world, even though it is the first two rules that stop most wannabe writers. And the fourth rule also stops writers who can finish something from becoming professional writers.

Everybody in this modern world looks for ways and reasons around this rule. That's how ingrained the modern myth of rewriting is in our culture.

One good thing right off about this rule: If you don't rewrite, just get it correct the first time through, you have more time to write new stories. And writers are always pressed for time.

Yet, time seems to make no difference to writers having trouble with this rule.

Rule #3 is actually an offshoot of Rule #2 failure.

Rule #2 is that you must finish what you write. If you are rewriting, you are not finishing.

And this rule plays right smack into every beginning writer's fear that what they wrote isn't good enough.

(Personally, I'm not sure where the thinking comes from that if they couldn't get it correct the first time, why looking at it and stirring the words around will make it better, but that is the myth.)

So there is a lot to this rule.

And people are always wondering what Heinlein really meant.

Well, he meant exactly what he wrote. You must refrain from rewriting unless to editorial order.

Period.

That simple.

So let me break the rule down into the three parts and try to show how some of these parts work and why they fit just fine in the modern world if you actually follow the rule as Heinlein intended.

Part One…You Must Refrain

Part Two…Rewriting

Part Three…Unless to Editorial Order

Part One of Rule #3…
You Must Refrain

Heinlein, at the time he wrote this, was talking to beginning writers about what they were hearing about writing. At the time, in 1947, university programs were booming because of the GI Bill and so many WWII vets going back to school.

English teachers by this point in time had bought completely into the articles published in the late 1800s about how writing slowly would make better literature.

And at the same time writers such as Hemingway were tired of all the new-writer questions as being stupid. Everyone knew Hemingway was a reporter who wrote one-draft fast articles and books. He had made that clear.

Yet he still kept getting the same questions, as all experienced writers get, from wave after wave of new writers. So he started making stuff up about how he wrote, making it so outlandish that he was sure that writers would just laugh and realize they were being made fun of.

Of course, new writers have no sense of humor, so generations of new writers wrote standing up and did thirty or forty drafts because Hemingway told them to. It was a joke, folks.

So when Heinlein wrote his article and gave his five business rules, he was in a way trying to tell the truth to young writers to fight the idiocy coming out of Hemingway's jokes.

So the phrase "You must refrain…" means exactly that. Do not think about a second draft. Just flat don't do them.

Get it right the first time through. Just refrain from what some writers were saying in jokes and English teachers were spreading around to get writers to slow down so they didn't have to read as much.

Also, at the point Heinlein wrote this, the pulp magazines and digests were still going strong and building circulation again after the war. Writers wrote for 1 cent per word on typewriters. As one major pulp writer said when asked, "They don't pay me to rewrite."

Part Two of Rule #3…Rewriting

What is rewriting? Wow, can't tell you how often I get that question and writers want me to define it right down to how much they can and can't touch.

Well, first let me tell you what rewriting is not. Got that?

Rewriting is not:

—Fixing errors
—Fixing typos
—Fixing wrong details

If you want to know how Heinlein and other major one-draft writers used to do it, simply find online some of their pages of manuscripts. I am sure the pages put online will be the most marked up, but that's fine as well.

What those of us who started with typewriters knew was that you could fix mistakes on a page before mailing it. Up to ten mistakes before you had to retype the page. That's why the manuscript format is double spaced, so there is room between lines to add in words or even a sentence.

Most of Heinlein's manuscripts have a hand correction about every page of a detail fixed. At least the manuscripts I have seen.

I've also seen a lot of Harlan Ellison manuscripts. You know he wrote one draft on a typewriter in store windows and posted each page as he finished it. I was also his publisher for a time and his manuscripts are very clean, usually only one or two word corrections a page.

You get the story correct the first time, but you can fix typos, spelling, and wrong details.

That's what Heinlein meant.

That's what I mean.

It really is that simple.

Creative vs. Critical Voice

Over the years I have spent a lot of time talking about the difference between writing in creative voice and writing in critical voice.

Critical voice is that voice in your head that says everything is shit. That your story is bad, that you must fix it.

That's critical voice. Nothing good ever comes from critical voice. Critical voice wants to make your stuff the same and safe and dull.

Creative voice is that surprising place where nifty stuff just springs forth.

Professional writers have learned to leave that creative voice alone and let it work. We do everything in our power to stay out of its way and then not change what it has produced (other than fixing typos and small details).

—Rewriting comes from the thought, "I need to fix that before it goes out."

That's critical voice and it is almost always wrong. When you hear that, just fix the typos and mail the story or publish it and move on.

—Rewriting is also caused by sloppy first drafts. Somewhere over the last twenty or thirty years, a deadly saying has cropped up. "Get it down, then fix it."

This makes writing from creative voice almost impossible.

Think of your creative voice as a two-year-old kid. If you tell that voice that it can do what it wants, but it won't matter, parents (critical voice) will just make it better later, the kid won't want to play at all.

But if you follow Heinlein's 3rd rule and promise your creative voice you won't touch what the creative voice comes up with, you will be amazed at how freeing that is and how much original and unique work comes out.

The idea of sloppy writing is just such a waste of time.

Basically, when Heinlein said, "You must refrain from rewriting…" he was telling new writers to work to get it right the first time through.

Yeah, yeah, I know, that's not what your English teacher told you.

That's not the myth.

So keep doing many, many drafts, maybe as many as Hemingway told you to do, and remain an aspirant as Heinlein said.

Also remember, if you are rewriting things all the time, you are not finishing anything and Rule #2 has got you in its grips.

Part Three of Rule #3…
Unless to Editorial Order

This used to be such a forgotten part of this rule for decades. It was obvious.

If you mailed off your story or novel to a major editor and the editor asked for a rewrite to fix something to help the story fit their magazine or book line better, then you considered it.

You might do it, you might decline.

Harlan Ellison added to Heinlein's rule…"And then only if you agree."

All of that still applies.

But this new world has really confused things for this last little clause of rule #3.

First off, agents are not editors.
Duh.

Yet beginning writers will rewrite and rewrite and rewrite for agents who can't write a check or even have a clue what they are doing.

I'll be honest, and I have talked about it a number of times on my blog, this practice is the stupidest thing I have ever seen in publishing.

Period.

If you are trapped in such stupidity, here is my suggestion:

Stop!!!

Withdraw the book and move on. Go back to your first original draft and trust your own writing and voice. Act like an artist instead of a doormat for heaven's sake.

Second, some scam book doctors you pay are not editors.

If you pay someone, they are NOT AN EDITOR. They can't write you a check. In fact, you are paying them so you can be scammed and your book ruined.

Unless this editor has published fifty or more novels, just STOP!!!

Withdraw the book, count the money spent as learning, and start trusting your own voice and writing. Again, act like an artist.

Again, the only exception to this is if the book-doctor/editor is a major published writer and knows what they are talking about.

But most writers go to "editors" who have published a couple how-to-write scam books.

Seriously?

Think, people, just think.

So what to do with Heinlein's Rule #3?

Follow it.

Completely.

Write the best story or book you can the first time through.

Fix typos and spelling mistakes.

Give the book to a trusted first reader, then fix the nits they find.

Then move on to rule #4.

Yup, that simple.

And really, really that hard in this world of rewriting myths.

As Heinlein said, these rules look simple and are almost impossible to follow.

Why are they impossible to follow? Because simply, you won't let yourself follow them.

You are the only person stopping yourself.

And think about how much more fun you'll have writing if you don't rewrite.

And how much more time you'll have to play with new stories.

CHAPTER SIX

Continuing with the third rule.

Rule #3: You Must Refrain from Rewriting Unless to Editorial Order.

I wanted to go at this rule one more time to make sure I've been clear. Most of the time, in this modern world, rewriting is when you do a sloppy first draft with the intent of "letting it sit" (dumbest thing I have ever heard) and then "fix it" later.

That assumes, of course, that your story is broken.

And that you have suddenly gained a vast amount of new skills since doing the story the first time.

I will often get comments from writers in workshops when I say, "Great job. It works fine." The writer wants to know what is wrong. If I don't say anything is wrong, nothing is wrong.

That kind of thinking, of always thinking something is broken, comes directly out of this myth that everything must be rewritten because it is clearly broken.

If you tell your creative voice to do it right the first time, the story won't be broken.

It might not work the way you feel it should, but it won't be broken and some readers might think it works just fine as is.

Cycling

This modern world of computers has allowed us to use a wonderful new method of writing fiction. That's called cycling.

The first thing you must understand about this new method of working in creative voice to create a clean story the first time through is that you, the author, are the god of your story.

You are unstuck in time in your story.

You could write the last line, the first line, a middle line, and then jump around filling in gaps.

The intent is to make a story that the reader will start into on page one, word one, and end up at the last word.

BUT YOU DON'T HAVE TO WRITE IT THAT WAY.

This is the hardest concept for a new writer to grasp after English classes. English teachers talk about the complexity and all that of fiction, and all of us thought that the authors must have been really brilliant to start from that first word and put all that nifty stuff in at exactly the right moment.

Nope.

You are the god of your own story, you can jump around all you want in your story and do anything you want.

As long as you do it in creative mode.

In the old days, writers would add in pages, or hand-write in sentences in earlier pages that needed to be added because of something that came later in the story.

I would often have a page that was numbered 3a that came right after page 3 in my story.

In our modern world of computers, we can cycle back in creative mode and just add in or take out what we want when we want.

How I do it (and it turns out, many other professionals I have talked to are the same) is that I write about 400 to 600 words (into the dark) and then bog down.

I instantly jump back to the start of those 400 words and run through them, adding in a detail, reading it, touching it, until I am back to the blank page with some speed and I go another 400 to 600 words.

Then I cycle back about 500 words and do it again.

If you graphed it, it would look like I am moving forward and then jumping up out of the timeline and circling back into the timeline of the story and then going forward again.

I'll repeat until I get to the end and the story is done and clean because I have looked at most of it twice. (I talk a lot more about this method in the book *Writing into the Dark.)*

I do this all while my creative voice is in control.

I average about 1,000 words per hour of finished story with this method, which always includes a five-minute break every hour.

Rewriting has been made easy with computers. That is the huge problem.

But cycling isn't rewriting, it's just using the computer tool to do what writers have always done. Jump around in time in our stories.

So remember, just because the reader will read a story from word one to the final word doesn't mean you have to write it that way.

Editors

Let me describe the types of editors there are in this new world just to be very clear.

Traditional Editor

This editor is hired by a magazine or a book company to put together a magazine or a book line. They have very specific things they are looking for and will often ask you to touch up your book, do a pass through the book to help it fit their book line or magazine better.

That's the kind of thing Heinlein was talking about with the last part of Rule #3. These editors can write you checks for your work.

Book Doctors/Developmental Editors/ Content Editors

All of these types of editors you pay are scams. (With the exceptions of major writers with long careers helping out younger writers for a fee.)

Granted, many of these book doctors have their hearts in the right place. I understand that. They want to help young writers, but the book doctors (or developmental editors or whatever you call them) have no credentials and could no more tell what makes a better book than your neighbor down the street. (Actually, feedback from your neighbor might be better.)

So they are actually hurting young writers instead of helping them.

Do not pay these book doctors. Just trust your own creative voice, your own art.

And focus on learning how to tell better stories over years by how-to books, taking classes, and listening to writers who have forty or fifty novels published.

In other words, learn from those a ways down the road that you want to walk and never grovel and pay someone with no credentials.

Line Editors

Line editors are editors who look for consistency in your story and your words. They look for clarity. Great line editors are extremely rare and most writers can get by without them.

Often great line editors are also buying editors for magazines or anthologies.

Copyeditors

Every indie writer needs to hire a copy editor. You can find them in services and locally from newspapers and such. Copy editors look for nits, mistakes, wrong words spelled correctly.

Great copy editors are priceless as well, but you must, as an indie writer, hire one. No manuscript should go into print

More WMG Writers' Guides
**from all your favorite booksellers
in trade paper and electronic editions**.

without a good copy editor looking at it.

I am posting this book on my blog in rough form. It will be run through a copy editor before it sees electronic and paper print.

Copyediting is not rewriting. Copyediting is simply finding the last wave of mistakes and cleaning as many of then out as they can find.

But no book is perfect. None.

We all do the best we can and release and move on.

Summary of Rule #3

Heinlein was basically trying to help writers learn how to write a story, do the best they could, release and move on.

Forward.

Always face forward.

Think of your writing journey as a walking trip. When you write a story, you are walking forward, helping yourself by learning and practicing and creating more stories that might sell and get you readers.

But the moment you stop and turn around to rewrite something, you have stopped your forward momentum and actually walked backwards to hurt your fiction.

Forward.

Always face and move forward.

The modern world has developed this fantastically powerful myth that all writing must be rewritten to be good. And no writer coming into fiction writing is immune from the pressure of the myth.

Writing is an art.

Good stories come from the creative side of our minds. To tell good stories, you must train that creative side to let go and play.

Write the story, finish the story, release the story. Rules 1-3.

It really is as simple as Heinlein said.

But in this modern world, it is really that hard.

CHAPTER SEVEN

On to the fourth rule.

Rule #4: You Must Put It on the Market.

"It" in the rule refers to your finished and not rewritten story or novel.

On the surface, this rule is very, very basic. And yet it was this rule that I had the most problem with over the years.

This and Rule #5.

Old Traditional Publishing World

What Heinlein meant when he wrote this business rule in 1947 was that you had to send your story to some market that would buy it, publish it, and pay you money.

When I started with these rules in 1982, the meaning was exactly the same. So I started off writing, finishing, and mailing a short story every week to a magazine or anthology that might buy it. I did the writing on an electric typewriter and I didn't rewrite. (I did fix typos.)

I did 44 stories that first year, 43 the second year (while working three jobs), and was selling regularly by the end of the start of the second year. In fact, by the end of the second year, I had 16 short-story sales.

This was all fine and swell and nifty as long as I was only writing short stories. But then I started writing novels.

I still wrote short stories following Heinlein's Rules, but I would often just show them to Kris and then never get around to mailing them.

Over the years, knowing I had this problem, I started a number of things that were designed to help me follow this rule.

One solution was called "The Race."

The Race was simple. You got one point for every short story you had in the mail to a market (remember, this was pre-indie world), three points for every chapter and outline you had out, and eight points for every full novel you had under submission.

I managed just over 70 different short stories in the mail at the same time during the years the race was going on in my writer magazine called *The Report*.

I was not leading the race.

Kevin J. Anderson and Kristine Kathryn Rusch were always ahead of me in points.

It is amazing, looking back at those old issues of *The Report* from the late 1980s, that the names that were on the top of The Race ended up with long careers and the names that only had a few stories out in the race aren't around anymore.

Heinlein said, "You must put it on the market."

But chances are the writers at the bottom of The Race during those years had issues with the first three rules. Kevin, Kris, and I had no issue with those first three. And The Race was a fun way to help us all keep stuff out.

Actually, it helped me.

But to this day, I still find stories that I never mailed.

Wonder why I never sold the stories, huh?

But for the most part, I managed to keep on Rule #4.

The New World of Publishing

Wow, do authors today have more choices for their stories and novels than Heinlein did in 1947.

Or what I did in 1982.

A ton more.

But the meaning of Rule #4 remains solid.

When you finish a story or novel, you must put it on the market.

But what does "market" mean in this modern world?

Well, for short fiction, the traditional rules still work fine. In fact, this is a new golden age for short fiction with as many magazines publishing fiction now as in the 1940s.

So mailing short stories to traditional magazines like I did in the 1980s and 1990s still works great. And I recommend it with short fiction.

As far as mailing novels into the traditional publishing world, I DO NOT recommend it at the moment. Contracts are very bad, advances are so low as to be laughable, and it takes too long for anything to get to readers who have grown used to getting it Now!

Want to know an interesting bit about Heinlein in his day? Novels were mostly sold to pulp magazines. And ended up in books later, if they were lucky.

When I started writing and mailing novels in the mid-1980s, you sent your work directly to book editors and often sold the editors projects over lunch at conventions.

Those days, both Heinlein's and my early days, are long gone.

For now, stay away from traditional book publishers and their lackey agents. You will be glad you did.

Sending a book to an agent IS NOT PUTTING IT ON THE MARKET.

Sorry. Agents can't write you a check for your work.

Agents are not a market.

Indie Publishing

The new world of indie publishing has exploded since 2009. Now a writer, with some learning, can get a book copyedited and to readers within a month or so from finishing it.

Writers now deal directly with readers.

Getting a book or story out for sale to readers is putting it on the market.

In fact, that is the clear, bottom line of the word "market." Readers are the end product of all storytelling.

Readers are the market.

So Rule #4 now has many, many choices for writers. And that's a good thing. Stressful at times, sure, but a good thing.

For example, in July of 2015, I decided to write a short story per day. It was great fun and I actually did 32 short stories in 31 days.

I followed Heinlein's first three rules to the letter.

But what was I going to do for Rule #4 with those 32 short stories?

First off, I put them all together, plus the blog each night about the process of writing the stories, did a cover for each story, a blurb for each story, and put them all in a book called *Stories from July* that came out just two months after I finished the last story.

So in two months all the short stories were all on the market.

I will be, in 2016, putting some of those stories into my magazine called *Smith's Monthly.* (I usually have four or five stories per issue every month.)

A second market for many of the stories I wrote in July.

I will also be putting many of the stories in short-story collections over the next few years.

A third market for many of them.

And each story will be for sale in 2016 as a standalone story for readers to buy.

A fourth market for all of them.

For a person who has had a lot of trouble over the decades with Rule #4, I'm pretty proud of what I am doing now when it comes to this rule. I think I have finally managed, after over three decades, to wrestle this simple-sounding rule to the ground.

Finally.

Must Talk About Fear

Now, this is a problem area I have observed when it comes to this rule. And I know it is real.

But I have no deep understanding of the problem. My reason for not mailing a story was just laziness or lack of organization or a bad memory that I had even written the story.

But for some reason, many writers are flat afraid to mail their work to editors or indie publish their work.

I guess writers feel that the editor or reader might hate their work and do some sort of mortal damage to the writer.

I guess.

Damned if I know. Just seems really silly to me.

So, let me tell you the reality, folks.

Readers (not jerky critics) don't read or buy something they don't like.

Editors don't read or buy something that doesn't fit what they are looking for.

Over my decades of editing, I can't begin to remember the stories I have bought, which means I loved them and worked with the author and paid the author money.

Why would any author think an editor who only glances at a story, knows it won't work, and passes on it, will remember the author?

Or the story?

Ego. Wow.

I think this fear might come from "my manuscript is my baby" problem some writers have. And of course, every editor's desk is empty, just waiting for the writer's baby to appear in front of the editor so the editor can take their time reading it and remembering every blessed word.

Ego.

But editors don't work that way.

And neither do readers. Even if your wonderful cover catches them, your perfect, active blurb draws them in, if the opening of your book or story doesn't work, the reader will move on and not buy it or read it.

And they won't remember the writer.

Readers are the ultimate editors.

So this fear of mailing is just damn silly on the face and under the surface.

Get over it.

Get over yourself.

Follow the fourth rule.

Summary of Rule #4

"You must put it (your story or novel) on the market."

Very simple, yet scary hard for many to do.

My only suggestion is to figure out systems that work for you to get the story from your computer and on the way to a magazine editor or a reader who can buy it.

And if your system breaks down, change it, fix it, get the stories out there.

Get past the fear, get past your ego, and just do it.

Rule #1 stops a vast majority of people who dream of writing.

Rule #2 stops a vast majority of the people who make it past Rule #1.

Rule #3 destroys stories and sends the writers back into Rule #2 problems.

Rule #4 stops careers of a vast majority of the writers who did make it past the first three rules.

And in the next chapter, Rule #5 wipes out even more.

As Heinlein said, these are simple rules. Deadly if not followed, but simple to understand.

CHAPTER EIGHT

On to the fifth rule.

Rule #5: You Must Keep It on the Market Until Sold.

"It" in the rule refers to your story or novel.

In 1947, when Heinlein wrote this rule, for the most part the only markets were pulp magazines. Paperbacks were just gaining strength and hardback publishers were very, very selective.

So all short stories and most novels were sold to pulp magazines, and the few digest magazines that were starting up, and maybe to the slick magazines such as *Saturday Evening Post*, if you were good and well-known as a writer.

But as with today, there were enough markets in 1947 to make this fifth rule a great business rule.

There are a million stories over the decades of how many times some book or story was rejected before being bought.

I had one story rejected over thirty times before finally selling it to a top market I had never thought of before.

I was following Heinlein's Rules.

Indie Publishing

The new world of indie publishing causes this rule to change slightly to follow Heinlein's intent.

If you put a story up for sale indie, the rule basically means leave it there.

I have heard of so many writers who, for some reason unknown to my way of thinking, gave up on a story or novel because it didn't sell to some preconceived level and pulled the story down.

And never put the story or novel back up.

In the old traditional days, we used to have a saying: "No story sold while sitting in your top drawer."

So, these writers pull down an indie-published story, give up on a story, usually out of fear, and put the story in a drawer. No reader will ever buy it.

Headshaking in this modern world of unlimited shelf space.

So this rule (in this new world) means get the story available to readers and leave it there.

Giving Up

The new world of indie publishing also causes another major problem with this rule that I see and hear about all the time.

It goes like this for short stories:

Writer: I've tried the short story at three markets. I'm going to indie publish it now.

Me: (Thinking) *Dumb.*

I never say that to any writer with my out-loud voice. But I think it.

For a short story, the advantages of selling to major magazines or top anthologies is far, far greater in both money and exposure and free advertising.

Sure, at some point you don't want to go below a 5-cent-per-word market, but wow are there a lot of that level markets out there.

It goes like this for novels:

Writer: I've tried the novel at three agents for two years and rewritten it twice for agents. I'm going to indie publish it now.

Me: (Thinking) *Dumb that you sent the novel there in the first place. You wasted all those years never putting it on the market.*

I never say that to any writer with my out-loud voice. But I think it.

Oh, wow, do I think it.

Agents are not a market.

So the new world of indie publishing is causing, with Rule #5, writers to stay up on the business, to find top short-fiction markets, to watch what is happening with the major book publishers, and to learn how to indie publish their own work.

That is all good, if you do it.

Boiling Rule #5 Down

Simple. Keep the story or novel on the market until it sells. For short stories, keep it going to the top short-fiction magazines. For novels, get it indie published and then leave it alone for a few years.

And if you have to touch it after a few years, do a better cover, learn how to write better blurbs, and make sure your formatting is working on all devices.

But past that, leave it alone.

Don't rewrite the story or novel because some reviewer said something. (Really the dumbest thing I have heard in this new world.)

Don't give up on the short story just because it has a few rejections.

Don't pull a story down from indie published because it only sold a few copies in a year.

Rule #5: You must keep it on the market.

For writers who have made it this far in the writing process, not following this rule will often swallow their work in self-doubt and wasted time.

Follow the rule. It's a simple rule.

Don't waste the time.

EPILOGUE

Robert A. Heinlein called these five rules "Business Habits."

I couldn't agree more.

Even though the first three talk about writing, they are firmly in how a writer manages his or her own business.

As Heinlein said, talking about the five business habits:

"...they are amazingly hard to follow—which is why there are so few professional writers and so many aspirants, and which is why I am not afraid to give away the racket!"

After following these rules since 1982 and making a living with my fiction writing since 1987, I can attest to how hard these five simple rules are to follow.

I would fall off, my writing would grind to a halt, I would realize I had slipped, and I would get back onto the rules.

Don't be mad at yourself when you slip off these rules if you really want to follow them. Just keep going at it.

A Few Additions That Need to be Made

First, you can follow the above rules like a perfect clock and they will do you no good if you don't continue to learn how to be a better storyteller.

Learning is critical because the business rules are guidelines to practice.

Learn, then practice, then learn, then practice.

Learning how to be a better storyteller is critical to making these rules work for you.

And that learning never stops. Ever.

Second, there is no place in the five business rules that Heinlein talks about speed of typing or production or all the

More WMG Writers' Guides
from all your favorite booksellers
in trade paper and electronic editions.

other favorite topics writers have these days.

You can follow these rules just fine if you only have ten minutes a day to write or if you have ten hours.

However, Heinlein's Rules, if followed, will allow you to have far more fun with your writing, something I hear that many writers have lost lately.

Third, you must keep up with the business side of the industry. Heinlein called these his "Business Habits." You need to also make it a habit to understand the new world of publishing and follow the changes.

The advice I gave above is for 2016, the year this book was published. I have no idea if the indie world will look the same in 2018, or if traditional book publishing will collapse or start giving writers their real value and decent contracts.

But whatever happens, follow the publishing business, stay up with it as best you can.

I hope these five business rules from the great Robert A. Heinlein will help you with your own writing going forward.

I know I owe my entire career to them.

And I still follow them.

Have fun with your writing.

~

New to the Thunder Mountain Series?
The first novels are available in electronic format or print at your favorite booksellers.

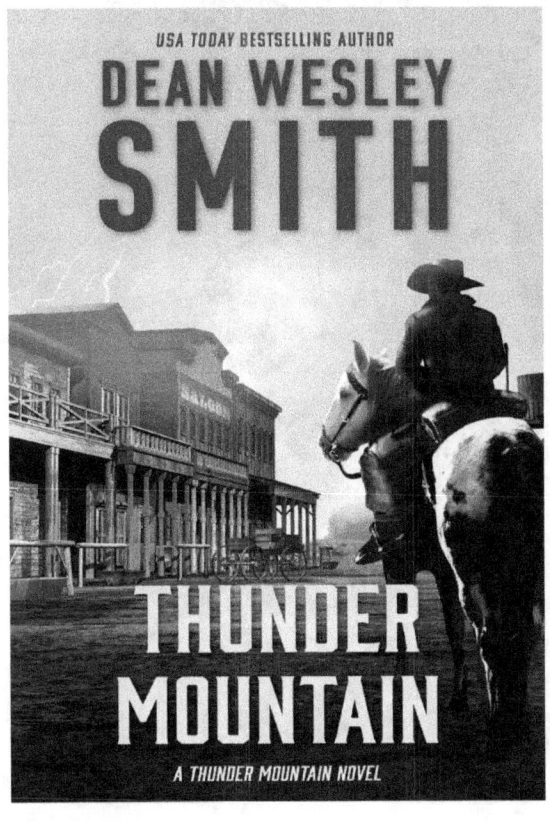

USA *Today* **Bestselling Writer**

DEAN WESLEY SMITH

*When the movie
Groundhog Day
becomes real for everyone...*

KEEP HOPING FOR A NEW TOMORROW

The planet and all time stuck at exactly 66 minutes.

Everyone finds themselves back exactly 66 minutes earlier, doing exactly the same thing as before.

Here and Now stuck at seven-ten on a Tuesday morning.

How would anyone handle repeating the exact same moment every 66 minutes? Find out in the most recent episode of "This is Your Story."

KEEP HOPING FOR A NEW TOMORROW

OPENING SEQUENCE
FADE FROM BLACK TO CLOSE-UP OF SPINNING GLOBE. THEME MUSIC SOFT IN BACKGROUND.

SUDDENLY A HAND REACHES INTO THE PICTURE FROM UPPER LEFT AND STOPS GLOBE.

MUSIC STOPS SUDDENLY.

CAMERA PANS UP ARM TO ANNOUNCER'S FACE AS HE BEGINS TO TALK.

ANNOUNCER IN SOLEMN DEEP VOICE:

The concept of here and now lasts exactly one hour and six minutes. Sixty-six very short minutes. Three thousand, nine hundred and sixty seconds. No more and no less.

ANNOUNCER PAUSES AND TAKES A DEEP BREATH.

CAMERA PULLS BACK FOR FULL BODY SHOT OF THE ANNOUNCER.

ANNOUNCER:

Here and Now became stuck at seven-ten on Tuesday morning, October twenty-seventh. Every man, woman, and child on the planet has handled the seven thousand, nine hundred and eighty-seven times that moment has been repeated in their own individual manner.

ANNOUNCER AGAIN PAUSES.

THEN CONTINUES WITH A BRIGHTER TONE IN HIS VOICE:

This next half hour we again bring to you another unique story of the moment time became stuck. So welcome ladies and gentlemen, your host for the eight hundredth live edition of THIS IS YOUR STORY, Martin Knight.

CAMERA PANS FROM ANNOUNCER TO WHERE HOST ENTERS FROM PARTED CURTAINS.

HOST MOVES TO SET CONSISTING OF TWO CHAIRS AND A SMALL COFFEE TABLE.

BACKDROP IS A LARGE MAP OF THE CITY.

CANNED APPLAUSE STARTS AS HOST ENTERS AND LASTS UNTIL HE HOLDS HIS HANDS UP.

"Thank you, Dick," Martin Knight says as the applause dies. "And welcome everyone to our eight-hundred-and-seventh live show without missing an hour."

CANNED AUDIENCE APPLAUSE

Martin Knight goes on. "Today, as a special treat, we have invited a man who not only has a story to tell, as we all do, but one who is also a scientist working on the possibility of time becoming unstuck. So welcome if you will, Professor Webber Stevens."

CANNED AUDIENCE APPLAUSE

Professor Stevens enters from the left side of the stage. He is a relatively young man in his mid- to late-thirties. He has short, light brown hair, a larger than average nose, and deep-set brown eyes. His smile is convincing and he doesn't look nervous as he shakes hands with Martin Knight.

"Welcome, Professor Stevens," Martin Knight says, "and thank you for spending this period of now with us."

"My pleasure. I thank you for having me."

Martin Knight indicates the two chairs and both men sit.

"First," Martin Knight says, "instead of beginning like we normally do with where you were, and what you were doing when Now got stuck, I would like to ask a few questions about your work."

Professor Stevens nods.

"What exactly are you and the other scientists at the University doing to find out what caused the world to be stuck in the repeating hour and six minutes of Now?"

"Quite a bit, I assure you," Professor Stevens says. "As with any problem, the first step is determining exactly what the problem is."

"We are stuck," Martin Knight says.

LIGHT CANNED LAUGHED

Professor Stevens smiles and goes on. "Figuring out how we are stuck. Then we can find the cause. And from that, the cure. In this case, because all matter in our physical universe repeats its existence of a certain point in time every sixty-six minutes, we have had to reexamine the basic ways we observe and think of our universe. Also, since the physical time cycle does not affect our memories and how we think, we have had to combine physics with metaphysics in our studies."

"Sounds very complex," Martin Knight says.

"It is," Professor Stevens says. "Add to that the problems of not being able to record any data for longer than sixty-six minutes and you can see that it has been quite a problem."

Martin Knight nods.

"But over the last five thousand periods, we at the University, as well as others from around the world, have come to some reasonably sound conclusions."

"Such as?" Martin Knight asks, playing the interested host role with practiced facial expressions.

"I'm afraid I'm not authorized to expand too deeply on the projects currently under way," Professor Stevens says. "But let me explain it this way. Time seems to act much like grooves in the form of never-ending record or spiral. Every sixty-six minutes, this time spiral returns to a point close to a past point in time. We feel that something, somewhere, caused a break in the time stream at seven-ten on Tuesday morning causing the repeating that we now are trapped in."

"Do you have any theories as to what might be the cause?" Martin Knight asks.

Professor Stevens laughs. "Of course, there are hundreds. The leading theory puts forth that a black hole moved into the area of our system, just close enough to cause the break in the time stream. I personally don't think this is the case."

"What do you think causes the fact that our memories and minds are not affected by this time break?" Martin Knight asks. "And the fact that we are not forced to repeat the same thing each hour as we did the first hour? Thankfully."

LIGHT CANNED LAUGHTER.

"It seems obvious," Professor Stevens says, "that our very beings, our souls as some people call them, are not attached to physical time limitations. Therefore, we retain our free will. It's only physical matter that is required to return to that same instant every sixty-six minutes. Right now, our problem is that our souls are attached very tightly to our physical bodies. That's just my opinion. Not everyone agrees."

Martin Knight nods. "That makes sense considering that the fastest-growing religion right now is the Groundhog Day Church of Tomorrow."

"Yeah, there is that," Professor Stevens said, shaking his head.

"Okay," Martin Knight says, "one last question before we get on to the real meat of the show. Do you see a solution being found in the near future?"

"I see a solution being found. I'm just not sure when. But, since we are now all basically immortal, we have the time. And, of course, the reality is that we have no choice."

Martin Knight frowns, then quickly catches himself.

"Okay Professor Stevens, now to the real question. What were you doing when Here and Now got stuck? As we say here, *What is your story?*"

Professor Stevens smiles. "You might say I was in an embarrassing situation that morning. I had stopped by a woman's house on my way to the University."

"Are you married?" Martin Knight asks.

"I was," Professor Stevens says, smiling.

LIGHT CANNED LAUGHTER

Martin Knight looks at the pretend crowd, smiling, and then turns back to Professor Stevens. "So you mean to say that you were having an affair that morning?"

Professor Stevens nods. "That's right."

"Tell us about it."

CANNED AUDIENCE APPLAUSE AND CHEERS

"Are you sure?" Professor Stevens asks, looking at the camera.

"We are very sure," Martin Knight says. "We want to hear every detail. Right, gang?"

He makes a motion to the invisible audience as if asking for their approval.

CANNED AUDIENCE APPLAUSE AND MORE CHEERS

"Well then," Professor Stevens says, shaking his head and smiling. "I was with this girl I will call Mary to protect her privacy. Mary is a very attractive natural blonde who loved to play this game she called 'Dive for the Gold.'"

CANNED LIGHT LAUGHTER

"I would hold up the sheet, make a noise like a submarine diving alarm, then bubbling noises. She would always giggle and I would crawl headfirst under the sheet yelling 'Dive! Dive!' I had just reached my assigned target when time got stuck."

CANNED LAUGHTER BUILDING.

Martin Knight contains his laughter long enough to ask, "You mean that you end up between this Mary's legs every sixty-six minutes?"

CANNED LAUGHTER GETS LOUDER

Professor Stevens smiles and nods and Martin goes back to laughing along with the canned laughter.

Finally, Martin Knight asks, "I'll bet your wife wasn't fond of this entire matter, was she?"

Professor Stevens' smile drains away. "She didn't find out for the first thousand times or so. When she finally did, she handled it for a few more times, then tried to move out. At that point, I was still making the fifteen-minute drive home every hour from Mary's apartment. Of course, my wife couldn't move out since she would keep popping back in every sixty-six minutes."

LIGHT CANNED AUDIENCE MOANING.

Professor Stevens went on. "After she gave up moving out, she tried not letting me in the door. When that didn't work, she took to killing herself with my deer rifle every time I would come home."

CANNED AUDIENCE GASPS.

"She killed herself almost a hundred times before I finally gave up and left her alone. I haven't seen her since. I've now

been going every hour to the University to work."

Professor Stevens looks up into the camera. "I'm sorry Alice."

Martin Knight coughs lightly, then goes on. "And what about this Mary? How is she taking the situation?"

Professor Stevens laughs. "Not real well at first. For the longest number of times, she took to slamming my head between her knees before I had a chance to move."

CANNED AUDIENCE LAUGHTER

"We finally came to an agreement and she now gives me three seconds to get out of her bed."

"Nice of her," Martin Knight says and laughs.

CANNED AUDIENCE LAUGHTER

"I see our time, and everyone's time for this period, is almost up. I want to thank you Professor Stevens for joining us."

Martin Knight reaches out and shakes Professor Stevens' hand.

CANNED AUDIENCE APPLAUSE

"My pleasure," Professor Stevens says.

Martin Knight turns and faces the camera directly. "I hope that everyone will join us next hour when our guest on THIS IS YOUR STORY will be Doctor Raymond Block, a man who has delivered the same baby over seven thousand times. Until then, this is Martin Knight telling everyone to keep hoping for a new tomorrow. We've had enough of today."

Martin waves at camera.

CANNED AUDIENCE APPLAUSE AND CHEERS

CAMERA PANS BACK AWAY FROM HOST AND GUEST.

SCENE SLOWLY FADES TO A PICTURE OF A WORLD GLOBE NOT SPINNING.

FADE TO BLACK

Now Available
from all your favorite booksellers
in trade paper and electronic editions.

USA TODAY BESTSELLING AUTHOR

DEAN WESLEY SMITH

THE ADVENTURES
OF HAWK

USA *Today* Bestselling Writer

DEAN WESLEY SMITH

THE WAIT

Henry, the oldest person alive, lived in a nursing home room.

A standard small room. Nothing special.

Getting a picture of the oldest person alive is a dream.

But living a long time might not be a dream. And the picture a nightmare.

THE WAIT

THE THICK SMELL of urine mixed with antiseptic filled the air as the nurse led us into the famous Room 341 of Hilldale Nursing Home.

Since I had heard of this room so often for so many years, I expected it to be bigger. Maybe have signs or something. But it was simply a nursing home room with one bed, a small desk, and a television.

The home of the oldest human alive.

Dan, my boss and the reporter on this story, went in first. I followed with my camera and pack, wading into the smell as if into a deep lake. I was soon over my head and finding it hard to breathe.

"Henry," the nurse said clearly as she moved around behind the old man hunched in the wheelchair. She stood there, her too-pink hands on the handles of his chair.

"You have visitors."

Henry seemed not to care.

His thin gray hair barely covered his age-spotted scalp. His wrinkled, brown hands rested on the arms of the chair and a thin line of drool came from the corner of his mouth.

His pants were thick around his waist, as if he had a diaper on under them.

He looked like he might be 100 years old.

The records had him at 185 and tomorrow was his birthday. By sixty years, the oldest human.

No one could figure what kept him alive. Some said he had been a scientist and invented a cure for death. Others said his family had been naturally long-lived. I had heard a hundred theories and had seen his picture at least a thousand times in magazines.

In all the pictures he always wore a gray sweater and gray slacks. Maybe even the same sweater and pants he had on today. I had never seen a picture of him out of the wheelchair.

I credited some of those pictures of Henry with my desire to become a photographer. Sure, they were nothing more than pictures of an old man. And I knew, if given the chance, I could get a better picture, capture the true Henry.

Now, finally, the day before Henry's 186th birthday, after two years of fighting to get permission to visit, I was going to have my chance to photograph the man who refused to die.

Dan twisted around so I could see his face, then wrinkled his nose indicating the smell. "Let's make this quick."

I nodded.

"Well, Henry," Dan said, almost shouting as he leaned over beside the old man. "Tomorrow is your birthday. How are you feeling?"

In five years of working with Dan that was the stupidest question I had heard him ask.

Even as a gun-carrying redneck, Dan was usually all right. We argued all the time and I kidded him about his flat-top haircut as much as he ribbed me about my long hair. But all in all, we made a good team. I hoped today wasn't going to be an exception to that rule.

Henry didn't even blink an eye at Dan's stupid question.

I motioned for the nurse to step back so she wouldn't be in the picture, then I knelt and focused the camera in on Henry's face as Dan struggled to think of something else to ask the oldest man alive.

The wrinkles and sunken eyes sprang into sharp focus.

My hands were shaking with the excitement. This was my big chance. If I caught just one shot right, my work would be on the cover of every major magazine and newspaper in the country.

But something wasn't right.

The picture didn't feel as it should.

I moved in closer, trying for the exact right angle.

Then Henry blinked, turned his head slightly, and looked up directly into the lens with his huge, deer-like brown eyes.

The look froze me.

No one had ever taken that picture of Henry, with his eyes wide open, the clear intelligence still there.

No one.

Yet I had seen that look hundreds of times over my years of newspaper work.

In the eyes of mothers waiting for news of their lost child.

In the eyes of convicts on death row.

In the eyes of families waiting at airports for a plane that would never arrive.

Now I could capture that look in the eyes of the oldest human alive. All I had to do was move fast.

Yet I hesitated, continued to gaze into those eyes, into year after year of waiting, year after year of nothing but a single room, a single chair.

Suddenly I knew I was looking into the face of what it truly meant to live forever.

I lowered the camera and looked at Henry directly, without aid of the lens.

I no longer needed the picture. I had the image locked in my mind.

And my nightmares.

The world didn't need to see that picture.

Henry nodded slightly, as if saying, "I understand," and went back to staring off at a spot on the floor.

Waiting.

I stood, tapped Dan on the shoulder, and shook my head.

He looked around at me. "Why?"

"No good," was all I could say as I turned and waded out of the smell into the hall.

I kept moving until I hit the fresh air and the crisp bite of mowed grass on a soft wind. The sun felt great against my skin, as if I had been in a deep freeze for hours.

Henry was waiting to die. His birthday was not a celebration. It hadn't been for decades.

His body was a prison. No matter how much I had hoped for this chance, I would not take a picture of him waiting a wait that cannot be measured.

I would not hold him alive in a picture one moment longer than he was to live.

It was the very least I could do for him. But I so wished I could do more.

I went out to Dan's van, climbed in and opened the glove box. Dan's revolver was there. Shells were in the box beside it.

It would be so easy.

I pulled the heavy weight of the gun out into my lap. For the first time in my life, the cold feel of a gun felt right.

I could do so much for Henry if I wanted.

I could do for Henry what Henry wanted, what he waited for every day.

I was still sitting in the passenger seat, holding the unloaded gun, when Dan got to the van.

He took the heavy gun out of my hands and put it back in the glove box. Then, without a word, he drove us away from there.

I never took another picture, never froze another person in time.

Over the years that followed, no one helped Henry.

And he just kept waiting.

Some Classic Dean Wesley Smith Stories
Available at your favorite booksellers.

BURN CARD

A COLD POKER GANG MYSTERY

DEAN WESLEY SMITH

USA TODAY BESTSELLING AUTHOR

Retired Las Vegas Detectives Debra Pickett and Sarge Carson think the solution to a very old cold case came easy.

Turns out, a little too easy.

And the deeper they dig into the old case, the more they uncover a very ugly side of humanity. And bodies. More and more bodies.

Another very, very twisted Cold Poker Gang mystery novel.

BURN CARD
A Cold Poker Gang Novel

Burn Card

The top card on the deck after the original cards are dealt to each player in a game of Hold'em poker. That top card is mucked (or burned) each time before laying out the flop, turn, and river cards, so in case it was seen, no one player has an advantage.
In other words, a card is burned each time to ensure the integrity of the game.

Author's Note:
The characters in this book are fictional and any similarity to any person, alive or dead, is purely accidental. This is a work of fiction.

PART ONE
The House of Mystery

PROLOGUE

June 12th, 1977
Las Vegas, Nevada

CATHY WENDT SMILED at her kid brother, Kevin, as he did his best to stand on his head against the wall in the hallway. Mom hated it when he did that because it left scuff marks on the paint, so this time he had taken off his shoes. Didn't much matter, the scuff marks were already all the way along the light blue paint. And every time Mom saw them, she got angry.

The hallway had a light blue shag carpet on the floor that helped Kevin with the padding on the top of his head a little.

Cathy thought it cute that a five-year-old wanted to be a gymnast when he grew up. But she had a hunch her little brother was going to be able to do anything he wanted as he got older.

He was that smart and that driven. And that was clear already at five.

She moved from her bedroom door to help hold his legs steady. She was five-five and Kevin, standing on his head, already came up to her chest. Wow was he growing.

"Now point your toes and straighten your legs and you'll have it."

Kevin did and she let go.

Sure enough, he held himself there for a good three seconds before tumbling to the carpet. He was smiling like he had just gotten the best birthday present ever.

"You keep practicing," Cathy said as she headed down the carpeted stairs.

Her mom was working on something that smelled heavenly for dinner already, even though it was only one in the afternoon. A pot roast or something that needed all afternoon to cook, more than likely.

Her mom was such a good cook, it was amazing to Cathy that she and her mother both kept as thin as they did. Luckily, Cathy took after her mother, not only with the long golden-blonde hair, but the thin, short body.

But Mom had her other issues. Cathy didn't want to think about them.

And clearly Dad didn't help. His job kept him away often at nights. Cathy hated how he came home smelling at times.

And what he made her do.

She put that out of her mind. It no longer mattered.

Cathy was going to miss her little brother and her mom's cooking. Not much else.

And she was going to miss the good things about her mom. Not the bad things, not the ugly things, but the good things. She promised herself she would do that, remember only the good.

Ben would be worth it.

He was her love. Her soul mate, as they were starting to call it.

She went into the large, bright kitchen and kissed her mom on the cheek. "Smells fantastic. I'm headed over to pick up Ben and then we're going to the library to research colleges some more."

That was the cover story they had agreed on for today.

Her mom nodded. "Dinner at six sharp," she said without looking away from the potato she was peeling.

"I'll be here," Cathy said, making her voice sound bright and happy as she took the car keys off the hook near the back door and headed out.

Now Available
from all your favorite booksellers
in trade paper and electronic editions.

"Bring Ben if he wants to come," her mother said.

Cathy said, "I'll ask him and tell him how good it smells."

Cathy didn't make it to dinner.

Not that one, not any dinner with her family going forward.

Cathy Wendt vanished into thin air.

ONE

June 10th, 2017
Las Vegas, Nevada

SOMETIMES SOLVING COLD cases was actually easy. Only sometimes, but clearly they had drawn one of those easy ones this time.

Retired Detective Debra Pickett just stood beside her partner, best friend, and lover, Retired Detective Sarge Carson.

They both said nothing. Just stared at the scene in front of them.

They were in a basement of a home near the University. The home had been built in the 1960s and had an unfinished basement with a furnace in it and not much else.

The floor was hard dirt covered in gravel and in one side of the large, extremely dry room was a wooden rocking chair that looked like it had been used a lot over the years from the wear patterns on the arms and headrest area.

A dried-up corpse of an older man sat in the rocking chair, his gray hair down over his shirt and his teeth yellow. His eye sockets were empty and seemed to just be staring.

The guy had on brown slacks that had stained from his body drying, a dress shirt with the sleeves rolled up, and his feet were still in his slippers.

If Pickett had to guess, he had been dead for almost a year and had mummified in the dry air of the desert basement. Right now, even though it was well over a hundred outside, the air down here held a fairly steady temperature.

And no moisture at all. None.

Beside her, Sarge said nothing, just stared.

She had seen this kind of thing before. Never helped the sleep for the next few nights, that was for sure.

Sometimes a case just sort of solved itself. Hard to imagine that might happen with cold cases that had remained unsolved for decades. But it did happen. She couldn't believe this was one of those cases.

At the Cold Poker Gang meeting last week, she and Sarge and Robin had been given a very, very cold case of a girl by the name of Cathy Wendt who had vanished almost forty years ago exactly.

Neither she nor Sarge nor Robin, Pickett's old partner when she was on the force, had thought they had any hope of solving this one. Neither did any of the other retired detectives at the game that night.

But they took the case file just to go through the motions.

A forty-year-old cold case seldom got any traction. Just too much time had passed, too many possible witnesses had died, too much evidence had been lost.

After forty years, nothing much would be left.

They all three knew that.

Plus the records in the 1970s were all paper. And more than likely most of the ones they would need would have been destroyed decades before.

Robin had just shaken her head and said to call her if they needed her help.

Her computer work was not much use for forty-year-old cases.

But Pickett and Sarge had both decided to give the case a day or two of legwork before tossing the file on the bar at the Cold Poker Gang meeting room with the other unsolved files.

They did get one break and managed to talk to Cathy's kid brother, Kevin, a dealer down at a small casino off the Strip.

He had been five when Cathy vanished and all they learned from him was how it had destroyed his family. And how angry he was at his sister for vanishing and leaving them.

For leaving him with "those people," as he called his parents.

Deep down angry.

Then he told them about how, when he was sixteen, his mother killed herself in her kitchen. His father, who was never home much anyway, had stayed away even more after Cathy vanished and vanished completely when Kevin was twelve. He had no idea what ever happened to his father and didn't care.

Mostly they learned how much Kevin hated Cathy for leaving him.

And that was all he could give them.

So Pickett and Sarge decided to see if the boyfriend was still alive.

The police at the time had interviewed Cathy's boyfriend, Ben March.

Turned out he was the one who had called in that she hadn't shown up for an afternoon date with him. He had gotten worried, called her mom, they had both gotten even more worried, and within a day the police were in full search mode since she was only seventeen.

They never found a clue for days until the family car was discovered at the airport. Nothing suspicious and the police had no idea who had put the car there.

That was long before security cameras in those sorts of places.

The missing person's case of Cathy Wendt went cold quickly after that and had remained that way for forty years.

Not one clue, no one remembered it.

It had been ten in the morning on the second day of them looking into the case when they had gone to Ben March's home and knocked on the door. The day was already hot and clearly the old home was hot inside as well.

The house had clearly seen better days. The grass hadn't been mowed in a year at least and was nothing more than a few dried weeds and dirt now. There was a notice dated last winter on the door that the power had been shut off.

The drapes were pulled so as they walked around the house they could see nothing.

They knocked on a few neighbors' doors to ask if anyone had seen the man who owned that house. No one had in a very long time.

And Ben's only car was still in the driveway, one tire flat and a layer of dust coating it.

"You thinking what I'm thinking?" Pickett had asked Sarge as they stood near their car and stared at the rundown and abandoned home.

Sarge had nodded. "He's in there. More than likely dead for some time."

They headed back to their condo in the Ogden and had a friend on the force to actually look at Ben March's credit cards and bank accounts while they had checked his history.

Nothing had been touched for almost a year and he had no employment they could find.

Pickett thought that Ben had also been a victim to Cathy's vanishing as much as

Cathy's family. He had dropped out of school the same time she vanished. There were no other records from the time that they could find on him. Looked like he had stayed at home with his parents until they died ten years later and he inherited the house.

It seemed, as far as any records they could find, that he had never left it.

"It's amazing how one tragedy can lead to so many others," Pickett said, shaking her head.

All Sarge could do was nod. Both of them had been detectives for long enough that they had seen this kind of thing more than they wanted to ever admit.

And they both knew that more than likely Ben had been at fault for Cathy disappearing. If he was dead in that house, Pickett had doubted their cold case would ever be solved unless he had left a note as to what had happened to Cathy.

Well, good old Ben did one better for them.

Pickett and Sarge got a warrant to go into Ben's home and they found him dead, as they expected, sitting in the chair in his basement.

And they also found Cathy.

Ben had dug up where she had been buried forty years before, just enough to see one of her mummified hands and some of her long blonde hair.

Then he had sat down in the chair facing her and stared at the grave until he died.

Pickett guessed that he had killed the woman he clearly loved.

Pickett figured it had been a crime of passion.

Sarge pretty much agreed.

Or as Sarge said, even more likely it had been an accident that he blamed himself for.

Turned out, at first glance as they dug her up, that she had a massive injury to the side of her head that more than likely had killed her. The injury looked like it could have been caused by hitting the corner of something.

The coroner who was digging her up had agreed that it looked that way on first blush.

Why Ben buried her and pretended to know nothing about her death would never be answered.

Sometimes a cold case was just easy to solve.

She and Sarge really hadn't had to do anything. Eventually someone would have gone in that house and stumbled on the same scene they found.

But besides the brother, there was no one left that she and Sarge could give closure to. And Cathy's disappearance had already destroyed the only surviving relative, her brother. He didn't seem to care that she had been found.

So they had been given an easy solution to a very old cold case, but unlike many other cases they solved, this one meant nothing to anyone.

They had found Cathy and no one cared.

And Pickett found that amazingly sad.

Someone should always care.

TWO

June 11th, 2017
Las Vegas, Nevada

Just as she did every morning, retired Detective Debra Pickett stood at the marble kitchen counter sipping on a cup of black coffee and watching as three cats chased each other around the living room and then back through the archway into what had been her condo before she and Sarge merged their two condos into one massive one.

It was amazing how fast the cats grew up. Just before Christmas, they had been kittens. Now, six months later they were all lanky, young adult, almost full-sized cats.

But still with the energy of kittens at times.

Nose, Pickett's black-and-white girl cat, couldn't get enough playing with Sarge's two orange tabbies, Pete and Ree. It was funny how Nose seemed to be in charge, acting above the two boys at times, and clearly controlling the games.

She was one smart little girl cat.

And the two orange boys were just sweethearts who purred at the slightest touch and loved to sit on laps when Picket and Sarge watched movies while Nose sat close.

And even as almost adults, the cats had more than enough room to play, considering that in the combined condos there were two kitchens, enough bedrooms to hold a small convention, and two full living rooms and dining rooms.

Pickett knew that having two penthouse condos connected was not how most retired Las Vegas detectives ended up. She was well-off financially from her divorce from the idiot who loved his secretary more than his money. But Sarge seemed to be at the next level of rich from money left to him by his parents.

As he had said one night, "Nothing to ever worry about."

Pickett sipped on her coffee again and watched the cat chase action as the three cats left the kitchen again at full speed, came back, and then disappeared up the stairs.

That was their normal trail and heaven help the human who crossed that

trail during the "running of the cats," as Sarge called it.

As with every morning, she had gotten up and showered before Sarge and had made the coffee. They had no plans at all for the day, since they had solved the one case yesterday.

If you call what they did solving anything.

They had just been first onto an awful scene, nothing more.

So today they didn't even have a breakfast meeting with Robin, the third member of their team.

This morning Pickett wore jeans, a light-blue cotton blouse she left untucked, and tennis shoes. She had her badge in a holder on her belt covered by her blouse and her service gun in a holster under her arm. She would hide that with a very light, blue jacket when they went out.

The jacket was long-sleeved to keep her arms from being burnt in the sun and she had a wide-brimmed hat to cover her head. She had such white skin, even the hint of sun often made her look like a cherry tomato. Amazing she had made it all these years in Las Vegas.

The weather today promised to be clear and hot. She could already see the heat shimmers coming off the buildings below their condo.

Sarge said he loved their routine of her going first in the morning and the fact that she never spent much time in the bathroom getting ready. His ex-wife, who had left him for another man, spent far too much time in the bathroom by Sarge's measure.

"Never could tell the difference if she took five minutes or an hour."

Pickett had socked him on the arm for that comment and told him, "Respect the work women do to look nice."

He had said he respected it, just didn't understand most of it.

Both of them had agreed that their marriages had been casualties of their jobs. It seemed that being a detective didn't leave much time and mental energy for making sure a marriage worked.

Sarge wasn't angry at his ex-wife, and said he even liked the guy she moved in with.

Sarge was far more forgiving than Pickett was with her ex-husband. Her ex deserved the young, blonde bimbo with massive bimbo-breasts, as she called them. Those two breasts had certainly cost the bastard a pretty penny in the settlement with Pickett.

More than enough to buy her condo, that was for sure.

Pickett looked at the empty countertop where they usually had the folders for their cases. She wished they had a case this morning. The Cold Poker Gang didn't meet for a few days yet, so they were case-less for the first time in a very long time. Felt damned odd, actually.

The Cold Poker Gang, made up of all retired detectives, met every week to play poker and talk cold cases. At this point, there were sixteen retired detectives in the gang, but only about ten to twelve showed up for the game on any given Tuesday. She and Sarge and Robin had decided they wouldn't miss a night.

And Sarge was the best player of the three of them, although Robin was getting better.

The poker and weekly conversations were fun, but what was the most important to Pickett was being able to carry her badge and gun again and feel useful, even after she had retired. Being a detective had been her identity and now, thanks to the Cold Poker Gang's special task-force status, she had that back.

She actually had been too young to retire, but the divorce had made her lose focus a few years back and question everything, including herself. Now she was barely over sixty and everyone said she looked younger. She felt younger, especially now that she was back working and living with Sarge.

Sarge said the sex helped with that and she certainly wasn't going to argue that point.

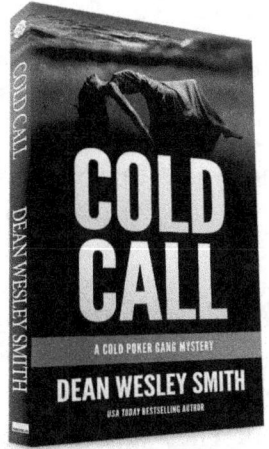

More Cold Poker Gang Novels
available at your favorite booksellers.

At that moment, Sarge came from down the hall, smiling at her. His hair still slightly wet from the shower as it was every morning.

He was the most handsome man she had ever met, she was sure of that. He had hazel eyes, thick gray hair, and a square jaw that gave him a superhero look at times, like he had been drawn right out of a comic book. This morning he was dressed in his normal jeans, dress shirt, and light jacket. He kept his badge where it always had been, on his belt on his right hip, and his gun in a carry holster under his arm.

Just as she did, he always put on a light jacket to cover the gun and the badge.

He kissed her, then picked up his coffee as the three cats, right on schedule, came tearing back down the stairs. This time the two orange cats were being chased by the black-and-white girl like she was herding them to their next part of the day.

As always, they stopped in the living room area and went to different chairs to take baths in the sun.

That was the end of the standard morning running of the cats. Now it was bath and then nap time.

Schedules. The cats lived by their schedules.

Sarge just shook his head and laughed at them, then sipped his coffee. After a moment he pointed to the empty kitchen counter. "Weird not having a case to work on."

"Very weird," Pickett said. "So what are we going to talk about over breakfast?"

"We may have to just sit and read the paper like normal old couples," he said, smiling.

"You calling me old?" she asked.

"That's going to take me a while to get out of isn't it?"

She laughed. "Buy me breakfast and I may let you live."

"Deal," he said.

THREE

June 11th, 2017
Las Vegas, Nevada

SARGE AND PICKETT had just gotten to their favorite table for breakfast in the Golden Nugget Buffet and Sarge was about to turn to the buffet when Robin showed up.

She was their third partner and Pickett's old partner from when they were both on the force. She topped the escalator and waved as she headed for the line to pay to get into the restaurant.

Sarge and Pickett had walked, as they did every morning, from their condo. The six-block walk from the Ogden had been nice, because it was early enough in the morning that the heat hadn't really set in yet.

Sarge had on a large cowboy-like hat that kept the sun off his face and a light jacket that covered his gun and badge. He liked the morning walks more than anything in his day, actually. Gave him and Pickett a chance to really just be with each other and talk.

And get a little exercise.

Pickett had on a big floppy hat and also a light jacket that covered her gun and badge as well. They just looked like an eccentric older couple walking on Fremont Street as tourists. Sarge liked that they blended in so well, actually, without having to wear the stupid shorts and loud shirts of the real tourists.

The buffet was separated from the escalator area by a wall of plants and fake windows. The buffet was massive, with tables divided into three large sections. Everything was decorated in golden browns and brass tones that blended nicely with all the plants. The place made Sarge feel comfortable and he really liked starting his day off here with good food.

Tall, floor-to-ceiling windows let in a lot of light on the far side of the buffet. Those massive windows looked out over a large pool that seemed to always be jammed in the summer. Along the windows was the most popular area for tourists to sit in. He and Pickett always sat on the far side of the restaurant, away from the tourists and closer to the plant wall between them and the escalator.

Allowed them to talk quietly.

He and Pickett both waved to Robin and then they headed for the food.

He got started his normal morning three-egg, ham, and cheese omelet made fresh, then while that was being done, he got some fruit and a muffin from the pastry area.

He took the fruit back to the table. Robin was still in line to pay, so he went back and got a freshly made waffle, covered it with syrup, and then picked up his finished omelet.

He really was hungry today.

Actually, he had been eating like this more and more since he and Pickett started working out down at the gym off of Sunset three evenings a week. They also used the Ogden gym room twice a week. He was feeling trimmer and leaner and often more hungry in the morning.

As he was sitting down, Robin finally got through the pay line and joined them.

Robin and Pickett, when active, had been known as the best detective team on the force. Sarge had heard of them far before he had gotten lucky enough to meet them after they retired. He couldn't believe his luck when he was assigned a Cold Poker Gang case with them.

The three of them had been working together ever since, and of course, he and Pickett were now living together.

Robin was solid, with shoulders like a weight-lifter, which she was not. She said those shoulders came naturally. She always dressed in a nice blouse and dress jacket that covered her badge and gun.

Her husband, Will, had the city's largest private security firm. He protected some of the most famous people in the world when they came to Vegas. And considering it was Vegas, he worked a lot. And Will and Robin were very, very rich.

"Scary rich," Pickett had told him one day.

Everyone in Las Vegas police trusted Will and his firm and his people. And the Chief of Police was one of Will's best friends.

Will and his people in his firm were amazingly good on computers and Robin was one of the best of them all. In the cold cases the three of them had worked together so far, he and Pickett had done the legwork while Robin did the computer work.

Sarge liked that arrangement. And it had solved some pretty impossible cases for them. Cases that had sat cold in police files for decades.

When they were working cold cases, the three of them often met here for breakfast. Sarge had no idea why Robin was here today.

"Missed our pretty faces, huh?" Pickett said to Robin as Pickett came back to the table with her food from the buffet.

"Actually," Robin said, smiling, "I did. And you know the case we sort of wrapped yesterday?"

"Sort of wrapped?" Sarge asked, looking up from his waffle. He didn't like the sound of that at all.

"Cathy Wendt," Robin said, "more than likely killed by her boyfriend, Ben, forty years ago and buried in the basement."

"Thanks for bringing that image back up," Pickett said.

Robin smiled. "Glad I missed seeing it, but you two need to go back there to that house after breakfast."

Sarge looked at Robin, not really wanting an answer, but knowing he had to ask. "And why would we want to do that?"

"Because," Robin said, "They found two more blonde girls buried down there next to Cathy Wendt, if that was Cathy Wendt's body."

With a smile, Robin turned and headed to the buffet to get some breakfast.

"Oh, shit," Pickett said.

Sarge just stared at his food, shaking his head. The case had seemed so easy, so simply solved.

But nope.

Now Available
**from all your favorite booksellers
in trade paper and electronic editions.**

He had a hunch this one was just getting started.

After all these years as a detective, you would think he would have learned that no crime was as simple as it seemed.

None.

FOUR

June 11th, 2017
Las Vegas, Nevada

PICKETT AND SARGE ate in silence, waiting for Robin to return with her food.

Pickett couldn't believe there had been more bodies down there in that unfinished basement. It seemed so logical that Ben had accidently killed his girlfriend and covered it up.

Open and shut.

But two more bodies showing up had certainly made that logical assumption a thing of the past.

Now they needed to know who all three of the other bodies were and why did Ben, if that was Ben, die in that chair, facing the bodies.

And did he kill Cathy or the other two?

Everything was now back in question. Everything.

Robin came back with two plates of food and placed them in front of her spot at the table, then sat down.

"I see that little bombshell was a hit with the audience."

"Bombshell is right," Pickett said.

"Stink bomb," Sarge said.

Robin laughed.

"So how did you find out about this and what is going on?" Pickett asked, staring at her old partner as she started to eat.

"Got a call this morning from Cavanaugh," Robin said. "He got assigned the case, wants us back in."

Pickett liked Cavanaugh and always had, even from the days when they were on the force together. He was a great guy, standard square detective build and tall, although he had thinned a lot since he had gotten older. He had a mostly bald head and bright green eyes and was whip-smart. He always wore a sports coat that looked far too big for him. It seemed to be his trademark. Cavanaugh called it "early seventies sloppy."

"Thought Cavanaugh was set to retire and join the gang," Sarge said.

"First of July," Robin said. "He pulled this case because with new bodies, the chief needed to keep it active, but the chief wants us to stay on it, so he gave it to Cavanaugh, since he is almost part of the gang already, but still on active duty."

"Yeah, he still has to do the paper-work," Sarge said, laughing. "He so loves that."

"So what do we know," Pickett asked, "besides what we had in the Cathy Wendt cold file?"

"Not much more at all," Robin said. "They have removed the other two bodies and Cavanaugh wants to wait for you two before he does a search of that house. They will run tests on all three bodies, including DNA tests, to see if they can figure out who those three are."

Pickett sort of sat back. "So none of them may be Cathy Wendt."

"We assumed it was because it being Ben's house," Robin said, "and the blonde hair, but there is a chance that Cathy may not be there. Chief has given permission to put a rush on a preliminary DNA test and two detectives this morning got a DNA sample from Cathy's brother."

"A rush on a cold case?" Sarge asked, clearly as surprised as Pickett felt.

"This isn't really a cold case any-more," Robin said. "A mass grave was found, so that warrants some extra."

"Are they still digging down there?" Pickett asked, afraid of the answer.

"They are," Robin said. "But the ground-penetrating radar doesn't show any more bodies."

"We can only hope it ends with three," Sarge said.

Robin agreed with that.

Pickett remembered what Robin had said about all three being blonde. That had to be important in some way, but damned if Pickett, after making such a bad assumption yesterday, wanted to even try to guess what that was about.

"Are the fine folks doing the digging going to have any idea how long those girls have been down there?" Sarge asked.

"They will get it close," Robin said. "Between the evidence in the holes like clothing and identification, we hope, and the autopsy, it should be within six months."

"That will help," Pickett said.

Robin nodded. "I already have a computer search running of girls with blonde hair that went missing before and after Cathy Wendt. It should be done by the time I get home and you get back to the house with Cavanaugh."

Pickett nodded and the three of them sat silently eating as the background noise of a busy Las Vegas buffet swirled around them. They just didn't have enough information yet to figure out which way to even start. Pickett had a hunch they might find some sort of trail at Ben's house in the search.

But until then, all three of them were just not speculating.

Finally, as they all finished, Sarge said simply, "Stink bomb. This case is a stink bomb."

Pickett and Robin both nodded.

Pickett agreed completely.

Everything about this case smelled off and seemed off.

And she had a hunch they were only getting started.

FIVE

June 11th, 2017
Las Vegas, Nevada

CAVANAUGH'S UNMARKED BLACK sedan was parked in front of the rundown old house. A police medical van sat in the driveway in front of Ben's old car and two other police cars were parked on either side.

Ben's carport that covered his old car had been taped off as a crime scene area, as well as the rest of the backyard.

Sarge and Pickett climbed out into the heat and both took their light jackets off and tossed them into the back seat of Pickett's Jeep Grand Cherokee before heading inside. There was no doubt that house was going to be hot. It had been hot yesterday when they first went in, and now, with the doors open, it was going to be cooking in there by noon.

Luckily, a thin haze in the sky kept the sun from pounding down too hard and the day was only forecast to hit just over ninety.

They signed in with the officer at the door. It had been a while since either of them had actually been on an active crime scene. Cold cases didn't tend to bring up active crime scenes that often.

The inside of the house looked like it had frozen in time in the mid-seventies. Old brown couches that looked like they might not support a person lined both sides of the living room. A large-screen television was on a stand on one wall and a newer, but worn recliner faced it.

There were knickknacks and pictures on the shelves on one wall and the floor was covered with a brown-stained carpet that looked, before it had a lot of wear, like it used to be shag.

The odor was of dry and rot and dust. Mostly dust.

The house inside was the same temperature as outside at the moment, which was warm, but not hot.

Sarge wondered if he and Pickett should get some masks if they started moving things around to guard against the dust.

At that moment Cavanaugh came in from the direction of the kitchen and the basement door. He was wearing just his dress shirt and slacks with a badge on his belt and a gun under his arm in a holster. Somewhere his large jacket had found a resting place.

He was also wearing a white breathing mask over his mouth and nose and white, soiled evidence gloves.

He pulled the mask to one side as he entered, smiled, and said, "You two just couldn't wait one more month before uncovering a pile of shit for me, could you?"

"We wanted you to enjoy your last month," Pickett said, going to him and hugging him.

Sarge waited until Pickett was done molesting the poor cop, then shook his hand.

Then Sarge said, "Hell, the paperwork on this alone is going to keep you busy for a month."

"Oh, god, don't remind me," Cavanaugh said. "Just the paperwork against an unknown estate to get a search warrant for this place this morning took almost an hour."

"Who is Ben's heir?" Pickett asked.

Cavanaugh only shrugged. "The title on the house says Ben March, but got a hunch that's as phony as they come."

"I'll get Robin on it," Pickett said.

"Thanks," Cavanaugh said. "Might save us all some grief down the road if we knew who really owned this place now."

Sarge watched as she quickly texted Robin the questions "Ben…heir??? And who really owns this house???"

"So," Sarge asked, "not finding any more bodies buried down there?"

"Three is more than enough," Cavanaugh said.

"So what are you thinking we should do, detective?" Pickett asked Cavanaugh, looking around.

"Grab a mask and a couple flashlights off the kitchen counter," Cavanaugh said, "put on some gloves, and each take a room. See if we can find anything that would give us a hint as to what happened in this horror house. Three bedrooms and a bath down the hall. Kitchen, dining, living area here. Back porch and the carport and a tool shed. I'll deal with searching the basement around the crime scene there and then work my way back up into the kitchen."

Sarge liked that idea. He had no desire to go back down into that basement.

"All right if we open blinds and windows to get more light and some air flow?" Sarge asked.

"Be my guest," Cavanaugh said. "Never saw anything in that search warrant that said we have to treat this like a damned cave. But forensics won't be here to go over everything until later this afternoon."

Sarge laughed. He really liked Cavanaugh and it was going to be great having him with the Cold Poker Gang.

A minute later Sarge and Pickett, breathing masks in place, gloves on, went down the hall to the two bedrooms on the end.

"Let's get the windows opened first," Sarge said, so they both went into the bedroom on the left. The room was dark and just to get across it they had to use a flashlight.

Two windows facing out over the backyard were there, side-by-side. A double bed was against the wall on the other side and a sliding closet door covered part of a third wall.

They carefully got the blinds open without stirring up too much dust, then managed to get both windows pushed up about halfway before the windows stuck.

At least the room was now bathed in light, showing off the swirling dust they did stir up. And there was a slight breeze going through the room and down the hall toward the open front door. Anything would help.

They went across the hall and pushed open the door there. Two windows looked out over the front yard and street.

They did the same, getting both windows open first so they could see the room, and the cross breeze between the two rooms increased.

Then when Sarge turned around to look at the room, he almost choked.

And beside him, Pickett gasped.

One full wall was covered in Polaroid pictures of a blonde girl. A large bed faced the picture wall.

From the one picture they had seen of Cathy Wendt from the file when she disappeared, Sarge would bet that all those pictures were of her.

There were hundreds of pictures on that wall, all clearly old, many yellowing as old Polaroid pictures tended to do. Most of the pictures were nude shots of a smiling, laughing young blonde.

"I think I'll let you take this room," Sarge said, starting for the door.

"No chance in hell, mister," Pickett said. "We do this room together."

Sarge stopped and laughed, then looked back at the wall of old pictures, some of them curling. A few had come off the pins on the wall and dropped to the floor. Clearly Ben and Cathy had been having a lot of fun before she died.

"And just when I thought this house couldn't get any creepier," Sarge said.

"Don't challenge it," Pickett said.

She had a real good point about that.

SIX

June 11th, 2017
Las Vegas, Nevada

THEY FOUND MORE shoeboxes of pictures of Cathy Wendt in the top of the closet. Most of them were of her clothed and in school or at a party or in a car. Some of them showed Cathy and who Pickett assumed was Ben together, laughing.

Cathy looked very young, from what Pickett could tell.

Pickett would check to make sure that really was Ben in those photos. As if they knew what Ben actually looked like.

She shook her head at that thought. No more assumptions with this case. A couple photos were of a meal with Cathy, what appeared to be her mother and young brother, and Ben. Pickett had no idea who took the picture.

It was clear that Ben had taken all the nude pictures of Cathy, right here in the same room. Only this room looked to have been his parents' bedroom.

That made no sense at all.

None.

And felt very creepy, actually.

"Very little left here from his parents," Sarge said, after they had searched for a while. "But I am thinking this was their room."

Pickett nodded. "I agree. I think it was as well. I'll text Robin to look into Ben's parents. We have no idea on anything here."

She quickly sent Robin a text that said, "Check out Ben's parents. Wish you were here."

Robin wrote back almost instantly. "Will do. Glad you are having fun."

Pickett quickly snapped a few pictures of the wall of nude photos and sent them to Robin with a message, "See if this is actually Cathy Wendt from the missing person's file."

Robin wrote back simply, "Yuck."

It took Pickett and Sarge a good hour to slowly work through all the stuff in the closet, spreading much of it out on the bed and piling some old clothes on the floor after they checked the pockets.

They all appeared to be a man's clothes.

Then they checked the chest of drawers and through all the clothes in there, pulling out the drawers and looking at the bottoms of the drawers for anything taped there.

Nothing.

They even got down on both sides of the bed and inspected everything under the bed and then along behind the drapes.

More nothing.

Only the pictures, the furniture, and men's clothing.

So finally they went back out to the kitchen to take a break, get some water, and change out their masks and gloves.

Sarge's face was covered in black streaks from the sweat and the dust and she knew her face was as well.

The house was slowly starting to heat up. Another couple of hours would make it into an oven, even with the windows opened.

At that moment Cavanaugh came back up from the basement and took off his mask, looking just as dirty and sweaty as Pickett felt.

"Any luck?" he asked.

"Not sure if you would call it luck," Pickett said. "We spent the last hour on the room on the right, both of us. Go take a look at the wall in there and you'll see why."

Cavanaugh walked down the hallway and into the bedroom.

Then about thirty seconds later he came back, shaking his head.

"No clue what that means," Pickett said.

"With luck, just kids in love enjoying sex," Cavanaugh said.

Sarge nodded to that. "The 1970s equivalent of sexting."

"But in his parent's bedroom?" Pickett asked.

"You think that was their bedroom?" Cavanaugh asked.

Both Pickett and Sarge nodded.

"Okay, from fun play to a little kinky," Cavanaugh said, shaking his head.

After a ten-minute break and a full bottle of water each, the three went their opposite directions. Pickett was really glad she didn't have to go back in that basement as Cavanaugh was doing.

She and Sarge did a complete search of the first bedroom they had opened up. Nothing at all and it didn't look like the room had been used much at all.

Then they went back to the third bedroom that was on the left across the hall from the house's only bathroom.

They opened the door to pitch blackness and a very dry smell of age and dust. This room had been closed up even longer than the other two. Even with the door open you could only see the outline of a bed and a dresser.

Pickett shined her flashlight toward the blinds and she and Sarge got the blinds opened slowly to hold down the dust and then opened the window to let the room air some.

When she turned around, the sight shoved her backwards right into Sarge.

The room, on all three walls, was covered in naked Polaroid photos of what appeared to be three different blonde girls. A different girl on each wall.

All of them sort of looked like Cathy, but were not Cathy.

And in the bed, on one side of the bed, covered up to her chin, was yet another dead blonde girl. Her skin mummified and dried, her eyes empty sockets. The blankets barely showed a dent where her mummified body lay.

She clearly had been in that bed and dead a very, very long time since her hair had fallen off her head onto the pillow.

"I'm really starting to hate this place," Sarge said, reaching out and taking Pickett's hand.

Carefully, making sure to not touch anything in the room even with their gloves on, they went back out and to the kitchen.

Pickett called down the stairs to Cavanaugh.

"First bedroom on the left," Pickett said when he showed up in the kitchen. Both she and Sarge had taken off their masks and gloves and were both drinking water.

Cavanaugh looked worried. He pulled his mask aside and went down the hallway.

"Son of a bitch" echoed up the hallway and into the kitchen.

When he came back down the hall he actually looked angry.

"We'll meet you here early tomorrow morning," Pickett said. "To continue the search."

"Thanks," Cavanaugh said, nodding as he pulled out his cell phone. "I can hardly wait to see what you two will find then. There might be bodies under the carpet for all we know."

Sarge and Pickett both laughed.

Sarge patted Cavanaugh on the back and then Sarge and Pickett got out of that place and into the cool air-conditioning of her car.

She had seen a lot of very strange and horrific things over her years as a detective. That bedroom ranked right up there near the top of the list.

Now Available
from all your favorite booksellers in trade paper and electronic editions.

Twenty minutes later they were naked, standing in their large shower together, trying to get the dust and grime and memory of that house of horrors off of each other.

PART TWO
Bigger and Bigger

SEVEN

June 11th, 2017
Las Vegas, Nevada

SARGE HAD SUGGESTED that they head out for lunch after their shower and a change of clothes. Pickett had called Robin and they had decided to meet at the Bellagio Café.

He just needed to be around some live people, some reasonably sane people, even though they were Las Vegas tourists. The image of that long-dead girl in that bed surrounded by naked photos of three young girls had rocked him.

Something horrid had happened in that house a long time ago. And not a bit of it made any sense at all. When they had first thought it was just a boyfriend accidentally killing his girlfriend and covering it up, that was logical.

But three more girls' bodies, all looking like Cathy Wendt, made no sense at all.

So getting out to a normal place, having some good food, and trying to make sense out of it all with Robin and Pickett appealed to him.

Pickett got them to the valet parking at the Bellagio in only twenty minutes.

The day had turned hot, but thankfully, they had to only be in the heat this time from the car to the casino front door.

The Bellagio Café was the casino's main twenty-four-hour restaurant, designed to comfortably seat hundreds at a time if needed. It had nice wood tables and booths separated from each other by rows of plants. Their favorite booth was in the back, surrounded on three sides by plants and against the back wall.

From there they could see the entire restaurant, have private conversations, and the laughing and bells from the casino floor were only a background noise.

They were already seated and had ordered two iced teas and three glasses of water when Robin wound her way through the tables and joined them. She was wearing her normal jeans, light blouse, and light jacket that covered her badge and gun. She was carrying a thin folder with some paper in it.

All three of them pretty much dressed the same in the summer.

"Cavanaugh filled me in and sent me some pictures," Robin said as she dropped into the booth and took a long drink of her water.

"Nasty, huh?"

Robin nodded. "Original police search missed the body because of the lack of electricity. They just opened the door, saw a dark bedroom, and closed it. Cavanaugh feels bad that you two had to find that."

Sarge laughed. "No he doesn't."

Robin smiled. "He wanted me to say that because he hopes you two will come back in the morning, early, before it gets hot, and keep searching."

Pickett laughed. "Kind of him to think of us. We told him we would see him in the morning."

"He said after finding that horror show," Robin said, "he wouldn't blame you if you didn't show."

"We'll be there," Sarge said.

"I told him that, too," Robin said.

At that moment a waiter came up, took their order, and left. All three of them were here so often, they didn't even need to look at the menus. Sarge kind of liked that about coming here. Made him feel like this place was sort of an extension of his home, and in a way it was. Just as the Golden Nugget Buffet was for breakfast.

"So did you find anything?" Pickett asked Robin.

"Parents are coming up as very strange," Robin said. "The Ben that owns that house has no heirs as far as I can find, assuming that is the Cathy Wendt Ben that was in that chair."

"Can't assume anything on this anymore," Pickett said.

Sarge agreed with that completely.

"The parents of the Ben that owned that place seemed to have existed, sort of, from what I can tell from the 1970s and sketchy records. But I am getting the sense they were all falsified records. Back then that sort of stuff could be bought."

"You thinking Ben lived in that house alone," Sarge asked, stunned, "back in high school?"

"My guess is Ben was a lot older than we thought he was," Robin said. "We won't know for sure until they get done with the body at the medical examiner's office. But records show that his parents bought the house with cash."

"So there is a theory that he lived there," Pickett said, "set up phony parents, enrolled in high school."

Robin nodded.

Sarge wasn't buying it. "Why would you jump to that conclusion on this?

I know taking those pictures of Cathy Wendt in his parents' bedroom was creepy, but that wouldn't lead to that kind of jump."

"Agreed," Robin said. "But here is what I have found so far from records that have been put online." She pulled a few sheets of paper out of her notebook and handed one to Sarge.

It was a high school list of students from 1977.

"I went to high school records first. Ben March is listed as a junior with Cathy Wendt."

Sarge spotted the names and nodded and handed the list to Pickett.

"The address of the house you found is in that school district. So as a lark I went to a second high school on the other side of town. Ben April is registered there as a junior the next year, a transfer in from Utah."

Sarge was getting a sinking feeling where this was headed and he didn't like it at all.

"Did a blonde girl go missing from that class in 1978?" Pickett asked.

"One did," Robin said, nodding. "I'm still culling out all the missing blonde girls I found from surrounding years and expanding the search a little."

"Damn it," Sarge said.

"I have a computer program running," Robin said, "doing more searches of other high schools in the area and in all of Nevada that correspond with a Ben being registered and a blonde classmate going missing. I'll know more after I get back from lunch."

"How did he register in another high school while his house was across the city?" Pickett asked.

"Don't say it," Sarge said, holding up his hand to Robin. "Just don't say it."

Robin laughed. "Ben April lived with his mother and father, who seem fake as well, in a home near the high school. The house is still in Ben April's name."

At that moment Sarge's bacon club sandwich arrived and even though it looked and smelled wonderful, he no longer was sure he was hungry.

EIGHT

June 11th, 2017
Las Vegas, Nevada

PICKETT WAS STUNNED at the pattern that was developing from just a little research from Robin. Robin was fairly convinced that a young guy by the name of Ben had registered in at least seven high schools from 1975 through 1982 as a junior. He had just used the month as his last name, starting with January and going through August.

From what little bit Robin had found, he was always a transfer in his junior year from another state. And for the April name, she had found the house that he had lived in.

They decided that after lunch Pickett and Sarge would swing by the April place, see if it was occupied, before ruining Cavanaugh's day with needing yet another search warrant.

But they still had so many questions.

Assuming Cathy Wendt was one of the bodies found in the house, which as far as Pickett was concerned was now a huge assumption, who were the other three?

From the other high schools, maybe?

Robin had a lot more research to do and she was pulling in one of Will's top computer people to help her, since so much of the stuff she needed was so dated.

And Robin was expanding her research to the University of Nevada as well.

Pickett had no doubt that at some point she and Sarge would be digging through old paper records. When you had crimes that were forty years old, that was the nature of the beast.

So after lunch, she and Sarge, with her driving her Jeep Grand Cherokee, headed for the second home that Ben March, or April, or whatever his real name was, had owned.

The place was small, as was the first house, in an old neighborhood that had seen much better days. It had been painted white at one time, but now looked a dirty gray. The house had no lawn and nothing but weeds surrounding it. An old, faded blue Toyota with two flat tires was in the carport.

Trash littered the driveway to the house and it was clear no one had lived there for a very long time. Sadly, it was not the only house on the street that looked like that. Not even close.

They sat in the car and stared at the place. Finally Picket asked, "Want to even try to see if anyone's home?"

She really didn't want to get out into the heat to even walk around the place.

"I suppose we better before bothering Cavanaugh," Sarge said.

Pickett agreed, but she had a hunch it would be a worthless venture.

They both made sure their guns were in place and their jackets covering them before they climbed out.

The hot air hit them like a hammer, not at all comforting. More oppressive.

A faded notice from the power company had the power turned off a long, long time ago. They wandered into the

back through the carport. The only tracks in the dirt were of cats and dogs.

No human tracks.

The backyard was full of trash and overgrown with dried weeds.

Most of the other homes she could see on both sides had similar backyards. One spark would level this neighborhood, of that there was no doubt.

They stood in the shade of the carport and Sarge called Cavanaugh.

"Got another problem for you," he said.

He listened for a moment and then laughed.

"No, Robin found another home that Ben owned that looks like the one you are in. Power off, no one lived here for year or more at least."

He listened and then again laughed.

"Want us to wait for you here? We are standing beside the house now."

He nodded and gave Cavanaugh the exact address for the warrant.

After a moment Sarge nodded. "What do you want us to order for you?"

Sarge nodded, then said, "See you there."

He hung up and turned to Pickett. "We're meeting him at the Burger King two blocks from here. The poor guy hasn't had lunch yet."

Pickett smiled and asked as they headed for her car, "Don't you miss all the details of being on active duty?"

Sarge shook his head. "Not a bit. Being on this task force is heaven. We get to be detectives and not do any of the paperwork. And I got a hunch this case is going to have paperwork."

"A ton of it, even if we don't find anything strange in this place." Which she was sure wouldn't be the case.

They got back in the car and Pickett got the air-conditioning going. Then for a moment they sat and looked at the house sitting in the heat.

"I don't have a good feeling about that place," she said.

"Neither do I," Sarge said.

Pickett stared at the house and then shuddered. "You get the sense we are finding an old serial killer's graveyards?"

"And each house is like a tomb-stone?" Sarge said. "Yeah, thought of that. Creepy."

"I think, from the looks of the pictures on the walls," Pickett said, "each place is more of a memorial."

"Serial killers like to take trophies," Sarge said. "The photos, the bodies, all could be that."

"But why keep a body in a bed and bury the other three?" Pickett asked.

"Real kinky," Sarge said.

Pickett laughed and then said, "More than likely that was the case."

But more than likely, there was a lot more to this than they were finding so far.

And that worried her more than she wanted to admit.

How much more could there be?

She knew the answer was a great deal.

NINE

June 11th, 2017
Las Vegas, Nevada

THE AIR-CONDITIONING inside the Burger King was working overtime, so the place had an arctic feel to it. They had already ordered and found a plastic booth away from others.

Sarge didn't miss needing to grab food like this while on the go on a case.

One thing he loved about being on the Cold Poker Gang task force was that they set their own pace. Cold cases seldom needed to be done quickly.

Cavanaugh came in, waved at them, and headed for the bathroom. Sarge could see that he was covered in dust and dirt.

They had just gotten their orders. Both he and Pickett had gotten two bottles of water and a milkshake each. They had bought Cavanaugh a Whopper with fries and a diet Coke and a bottle of water for later.

It took Cavanaugh a minute to emerge from the restroom, his face red from splashing cold water on it, his hair wet. But he was smiling. Water had dripped down the front of his large suit jacket and he didn't even seem to care.

"Wow, that felt good," he said.

Sarge shoved the tray with the food toward him and Cavanaugh nodded, took a long drink of the Coke, then dug into the wonderful-smelling fries.

"Get the new victim out of the bed?" Pickett asked.

Cavanaugh nodded. "Looked to be about the same age and height and such as the ones in the ground downstairs. Identification on all of them is going to take a little time, but the chief, with this fourth body, has put a priority on it in the labs. And we are all forbidden to talk to the press. So far, thankfully, no one has caught wind of this."

"What is the press?" Pickett asked, trying to be serious.

Cavanaugh laughed. "One more damn month and I can be on that side of that question."

So as he ate, they filled him in on Robin's research so far and how she had found this house and how she was searching missing person's reports and so on.

"Thanks for doing a drive-by before I went after a warrant," he said as he finished his hamburger and went back to work on what was left of the fries.

He took out his phone, checked something, then said, "We just got the warrant, so we're set to go take a look."

"Oh, joy," Pickett said.

Sarge laughed, then said, "Hang on."

He stood and went to the counter, got a glass for ice water, filled it half full of ice and then water and went back to the table with a pile of napkins.

"Put this on your neck," Sarge said to Cavanaugh as he opened a few napkins to their full length, combined them and dipped them in the ice water. "We don't want you heat-stroking out on us before you join the gang."

"After I join will be fine?" Cavanaugh asked, smiling as he did what Sarge suggested.

"Oh, we won't care then," Pickett said. "We're all old, remember?"

Cavanaugh laughed and said thanks. Then asked how much he owed for the lunch and Sarge waved it off.

Then he and Pickett both put the iced-napkins on their necks and Sarge filled the glass with ice and water again and took a bunch more napkins and they headed out into the heat and the second house, each carrying bottles of water.

The iced-napkins on the neck was an old trick Sarge had learned a long time ago to help with the heat. He had a hunch they were going to need it today.

Pickett parked in front of the place and Cavanaugh pulled his sedan into the driveway behind the old car in the carport.

Cavanaugh gave them gloves and flashlights and they redid their iced-napkins on their necks. Cavanaugh had called

in to the local cops what they were doing and a patrol car would join them shortly.

Then with Cavanaugh carrying a crowbar, they headed around back. No point in opening up the front door.

Cavanaugh first pounded on the door and yelled, "Police."

Then he cranked the door open quickly with his shoulder and the crowbar, pushing it in hard.

It broke off some rotted trim on the door.

Sarge was impressed. Cavanaugh looked big and wore a sloppy coat, but clearly the guy had kept himself in good shape as well.

Inside was pitch dark and smelled of dust and old air.

"Before we open the place up, let's do a quick search with the flashlights," Cavanaugh said. "Got any idea if there is a basement?"

"Robin said there was from the house plans she looked up," Pickett said.

"Shit," Cavanaugh said. "I'll take it. You two have fun with the bedrooms again."

"Thanks," Sarge said. "I think."

Then together, he and Pickett started down the dark hallway.

It was the last place Sarge had ever wanted to be on a bright, hot June day.

The very last.

TEN

June 11th, 2017
Las Vegas, Nevada

PICKETT INSTANTLY HATED this place. The house had the exact same layout as Ben's other home, if this actually was one of his houses. There had to have been thousands of these small three-bedroom homes built around Las Vegas in the 1960s and early 1970s.

Three bedrooms and a bath down a hall, a living room on the front half, a kitchen and small dining room on the back half. They had come into the small dining room area and there was a Formica-top table with four chairs, all pushed in under the table.

The kitchen counter was Formica as well and covered in dirt. Some really old dishes filled the sink, all crusted.

The door to the basement was off the dining room on the right of the back door.

Cavanaugh went slowly down those stairs as she and Sarge headed through the edge of the kitchen and down the hallway.

It felt as if they were almost under black water once they got away from the light coming in from the back door, with dust-motes floating in the air around them in the beams of their flashlights.

Picket could almost hear her own breathing.

"Start in the bedroom on the left," Sarge said.

"Okay," Pickett said.

All three bedroom doors were closed, so they opened up the door on the left at the end of the hallway.

"Damn it all to hell," Sarge said as he panned his light on the mummified remains of a blonde girl in the bed.

The poor girl had to have been dead for decades from the look of it.

Picket just wanted to be sick. This one looked exactly like the one in the other house. Blankets pulled up to her chin, blonde hair fallen around her head on the pillow.

How was this even possible that none of these girls had been found? Decades clearly had passed. Just the smell of a rotting corpse in a neighbor's house should have alerted someone all those years ago.

She and Sarge put their lights on the walls and the walls were covered with Polaroid images of at least two, if not more, young teenage blonde girls, all naked and smiling, clearly having fun.

And all of them seemed to be in a bedroom like the parents' bedroom at the other house.

There was no stress at all in the girls being photographed without clothes on. They were clearly enjoying themselves and in some pictures mugging for the camera.

Pickett left the room and Sarge pulled the door closed behind them.

The door on the right had an empty bed, thank heavens, but again the walls were covered with hundreds of Polaroid pictures of naked blonde girls.

"How in the world did this guy get so many young girls to take their clothes off for him?" Sarge asked. "And look happy doing so?"

"That might be the question that gives us some answers," Pickett said. But right now she had no idea either.

They again closed the door, then went to the bedroom across the hall from the bathroom.

Inside were more pictures on the wall and two blonde girls in the bed. Same scene, both with covers pulled up under their chins, both mummified.

Impossible.

Pickett couldn't believe they were finding this.

Just impossible.

They backed out of the room and pulled the door closed, then went back to the kitchen with the light coming in through the open back door. It was everything Pickett could do to not just go on out into the heat and sun.

Cavanaugh was just coming up the stairs.

"Anything?" Sarge asked.

"Gravel and dirt floor," Cavanaugh said, "and an old wooden rocking chair facing the open area like in the other house."

"So more than likely some bodies down there," Sarge said.

All Pickett could do was shake her head. She was numb. She remembered that feeling from horrid cases when she was on active duty.

Cavanaugh just nodded.

"We got three bodies up here," Pickett said.

"Three?" Cavanaugh asked.

"All mummified like the one in the other house," Sarge said. "Decades old at least. One in the back left bedroom and two in the bedroom across from the bathroom."

"And naked pictures of young blonde girls on all the walls of all three bedrooms," Pickett said.

Cavanaugh took a deep breath of the musty air, then started down the hallway to take a look.

"We'll be in my car," Pickett said.

"I'll be right out," Cavanaugh said, not turning around.

Sarge let Pickett lead back to the car and then get the air-conditioning running.

Then about five minutes later, Cavanaugh came out, walking slowly, clearly thinking.

He came over and climbed into the back seat and Pickett handed him a bottle of cold water they had brought from Burger King.

Cavanaugh downed about half of it.

"This has sure become a mess," Cavanaugh said. "Hang on and let me call the chief and see how he wants us to deal with this."

Pickett turned in the seat to face Cavanaugh in the back seat while he got in touch with the Las Vegas Chief of Police.

"The second house has bodies as well," Cavanaugh said. "Three upstairs, a chance of more buried in the basement. The bodies are as old as the first one. Mummified after decades."

He listened for a minute, then said, "Just me and Sarge and Pickett. Robin was the one who found the house, and she and her people with Will are still working on this. There might be more houses."

Again Cavanaugh paused to listen to something the chief was saying. Then he said, "We're sitting in her car out front right now."

"Understood, sir," Cavanaugh said and hung up his phone and held it in his hand.

"Well?" Sarge said. "The Gang shoved down the road on this yet?"

Cavanaugh laughed. "No chance you are going to get that lucky. Can you two meet me at around 8 at the first house

Now Available
from all your favorite booksellers
in trade paper and electronic editions.

tomorrow? We'll finish searching there and then come over here to see what we can find. The tech folks should be mostly done, except down in the basement, by then."

Pickett glanced at Sarge and he nodded.

"See you in the morning," Pickett said.

Cavanaugh started to get out, but Sarge said, "Hang on."

He made the active detective another ice-water pack for the back of his neck.

Cavanaugh put it on and said, "Thanks!"

Then he closed the door and headed to his own car, his phone against his ear.

"Have I said lately how happy I am that I am no longer active?" Sarge said.

Pickett laughed as she pulled away. "I think I've said it more."

And she honestly was very glad she didn't have to have the afternoon and evening Cavanaugh was about to have.

ELEVEN

June 12th, 2017
Las Vegas, Nevada

SARGE HAD SLEPT hard and was still feeling it as he headed down the hall from their bedroom and into the kitchen. Just at that moment, their three cats flashed past him and headed up the stairs.

"Almost died right there," he said, laughing, as the cats vanished from sight.

Pickett handed him a cup of coffee and kissed him. "Death by cat stampede. Everyone who has owned cats would know exactly what happened."

Sarge nodded and sipped on his morning coffee, trying to clear his mind for the day ahead.

The sun wasn't really even up yet, but the sky was colored with what promised to be a beautiful sunrise.

Yesterday afternoon they had gotten back from the second house after calling Robin and telling her what they had found, taken another shower, taken naps with the cats. Then he had cooked Pickett and himself a light dinner and they had watched a movie while sharing a large tub of popcorn.

Both of them fell asleep in the middle of the movie. He didn't have much memory of how they made it to bed.

Robin was going to meet them for breakfast this morning at the Golden Nugget Buffet, even though it was earlier than they normally got there. More than likely she had more stuff to share with them, but unlike most cases, on this one he wasn't sure if he actually wanted to know.

So far they had seven known bodies of young girls, all killed decades ago by some means not even certain yet. He had no doubt the body count was going to go higher.

He got a cooler out of the pantry and filled it with ice and then bottles of water from the fridge. Then he put three cold packs in the ice as well to use for their necks instead of using napkins, which dried out quickly and fell apart.

They drove to the Golden Nugget parking garage and made it up to the buffet in about the same amount of time as it would have taken them to walk. But this way they could leave directly from breakfast to head back to the first house to meet Cavanaugh.

Robin was already eating and the buffet had a slightly different feel about it because it was an hour earlier. This tourist crowd seemed to be in a little more of a hurry. More than likely to catch a plane or something.

And the big windows that usually streamed in sun were much darker. That changed the mood a little as well.

Robin had her carry bag next to her with her laptop and notebooks in it.

They waved at her as they headed to the buffet to get food.

Sarge stayed with his normal omelet and waffle and fruit.

After he and Pickett were both eating and Robin had finished, she brought up her notebook.

"How many more houses?" Sarge asked, deciding to get right to the point.

"Four more," Robin said, "for the high school years. All owned by fake parents and paid in cash for, all in bad neighborhoods."

"All still in his name, or fake name?" Pickett asked.

Robin nodded. "All had their power turned off about the same time a year ago for non-payment."

Sarge forced himself to keep eating. He had known the body count was going to go up. Now the question was how high.

"I'm hearing a lot left out," Pickett said, looking at Robin.

Sarge looked up as Robin nodded. He had never seen her so upset and tired-looking.

"I've been trying to track his money," Robin said. "Money is one of the only things that pretended to have a computer trail back then, so I figured I could help there."

"And…?" Pickett asked.

"I traced it all the way to 1975," Robin said. "When he first took the name Ben January and came into town and enrolled in high school, he was actually twenty-three years old, but looked much younger."

"You find his real name?"

"Benjamin Ronald States," she said, nodding.

That surprised Sarge. Robin was good, but how had she done that so fast?

"Originally from New York," Robin said. "Parents killed when he was seventeen and a junior in high school. He was an only child and his parents were very rich."

Sarge watched as Robin pulled out some notes. "He was dating a blonde girl by the name of Mindy when his parents died. She dropped him."

"Lost his parents, lost his girlfriend," Sarge said. "Ugly."

"How did you find all this out?" Pickett asked.

"Yeah, I am stunned," Sarge said.

Robin beamed. "Extreme high-tech facial recognition that Will uses for security, combined with high school yearbooks that are online. I wrote a program to scan all high school yearbooks for Ben, cutting down the points of similarity. Found three hundred on the first pass, then actually did a full facial recognition scan of those three hundred and got him. Took some high-speed processing and about six hours. Once I found him, I made a couple phone calls to old classmates."

Sarge was very glad all this technology was on the side of good at this point.

"Brilliant," Pickett said.

"Thanks," she said, smiling.

"So did he have a house here under his real name?" Sarge asked.

"He does," Robin said. "A beautiful mansion out to the north of town on a ridge. He owed a land development firm for the last thirty years and made himself even richer than he was when he got here. His hobby was nude photography. In fact, over the last three decades he has won awards for his nudes and his pictures are shown in galleries all over the country. He's that good."

Sarge just nodded and pushed his plate away. Pieces were coming together thanks to Robin, but they still had so many unanswered question.

And they still had five houses, more than likely with bodies in them.

"One thing I find interesting," Robin said. "There are no houses for January and February. March was the first one."

"One more thing," Robin said. "Benjamin Ronald States was married, still is married, for the last thirty-eight years, to a woman whose maiden name was Cathy Wendt."

"Still is married?" Sarge asked. He must have heard Robin wrong.

Robin nodded. "They are both still alive."

All Sarge and Pickett could do was just stare at Robin.

And Sarge knew instantly, from the look on Robin's face, that she wasn't kidding.

TWELVE

June 12th, 2017
Las Vegas, Nevada

PICKETT DAMNED NEAR fell over backward when Robin said that Ben and Cathy were still alive. How in the world could Cathy Wendt still be alive? And if this Benjamin Ronald States was the same Ben, what in the world was going on?

"Are you sure?"

Robin nodded. "But remember, I tracked him from his pictures, so there is a chance I am wrong on this."

Pickett nodded, reminding herself that there could be no assumptions.

"So now what do we do?" Sarge asked.

"We tell Cavanaugh," Pickett said. "This is an active case, so we tell him what we have found and get some police watching that Ben as we dig for evidence to put the guy away, if he really did all this."

"My gut tells me he didn't," Robin said. "Something is still off on the money trail and those six houses. I'll keep digging."

"And if Ben from the Cathy Wendt case is still alive," Sarge said, "who the hell was in that rocking chair in the basement?"

"And who are all the girls," Pickett asked, "both the dead ones and the ones in the pictures?"

Only the sounds of the early morning customers in the buffet answered those questions.

At that moment Robin's phone beeped and she said, "Cavanaugh."

"Morning, Detective," she said. "I'm with Pickett and Sarge and they are about to head your way."

She listened for a moment, then sat back, clearly stunned.

"I'll tell them, and they have some news for you as well when they see you."

She laughed, then said, "Sorry, but yes, more houses."

She nodded. "They will see you soon."

She hung up and smiled. "He hasn't had his first cup of coffee yet."

Pickett smiled. No detective after a long night should ever be talked to before a first cup of coffee.

"So what shocked you?" Sarge said.

"He called to tell me that all four bodies at the March house had been embalmed. And preliminary findings on the three in the beds at the April house are the same. They were embalmed a long time ago."

"Seriously?" Sarge said.

Robin nodded. "That's what he said."

"Well, that explains why no neighbors caught any smell," Pickett said.

"There would still be some," Robin said, "but if the bodies were left out to dry in the hot air and good ventilation, they would mummify very quickly in this dry air after being embalmed."

"Lott and Julia and Ander dealt with a millionaire serial killer," Sarge said, "who was embalming bodies and dumping them in a lake up in Idaho."

"They did?" Robin asked.

"I remember hearing about it," Pickett said, nodding. Lott and Julia and Ander were the three retired detectives who started the Cold Poker Gang task force. "Right before we joined the Gang."

"Happened while I was away from the Gang for a short time," Sarge said. "The killer was just using the embalming and a chain of mortuaries to kill his victims and make them disappear after he got done with them. Very different than leaving them in a bed or buried in a basement."

They sat in silence for a few moments letting the sounds of the morning buffet wash over them. Pickett was pretty sure she didn't want to know anything more about that case, especially after dealing right now with this one.

"Any idea how the girls all died in that first house?" Sarge asked after a moment.

"Blunt force trauma on the one, the first one they dug up," Robin said. "Nothing else, but the medical folks are just getting started and that will take a few days, including DNA, even rushed."

Pickett just sat there staring at the remains of the omelet on her plate, then pushed it away. She was no longer hungry at all.

"I'll get digging on those houses and the money trails from Benjamin States," Robin said. "See if I can connect him to those houses today. And see if I can connect an embalmer anywhere along the history of this mess."

"Those houses really are memorial tombs," Sarge said.

Pickett only nodded to that. And there were still four more they hadn't looked into yet.

And she wasn't going to.

Those could be left to the active detectives. She already had enough nightmares after two.

More than enough.

And they still had the first one to finish searching today.

THIRTEEN

June 12th, 2017
Las Vegas, Nevada

SARGE STARED AT the March house as Pickett drove up and parked. It now had crime scene tape around it and a guard sitting in a marked car out front. The poor guy had clearly been there all night.

Sarge remembered that kind of duty when he was first getting started on the force. Guarding a crime scene all night. Nothing got more boring.

Nothing.

At that moment Cavanaugh pulled up and again parked in the driveway behind the old car in the carport. Sarge wondered if anyone had searched that car yet. He doubted it. That was what they were here for today.

Cavanaugh, a massive cup of coffee in one hand, climbed out of the car, waved at them, and went to the patrol car to send the poor cop on his way home.

Pickett shut off her car and they climbed out, carrying bottles of water from the cooler they had strapped by a seatbelt on the back seat.

The sun was just breaking over the hills, giving the air a fresh, bright look to it. The temperature was still comfortable with a slight breeze, so with luck they could open up the house and get some air flowing through it before it got too hot.

"Just got active detectives headed to the other four house addresses I got from Robin," Cavanaugh said.

"I don't think I could take searching another one of these horror places," Pickett said.

"I'm feeling the exact same way," Cavanaugh said.

They went to the front door and Cavanaugh moved the tape and they opened the place up.

It smelled of dry dust and age and was far warmer than it was outside.

"Lab folks have been all over the place already," Cavanaugh said, "but let's still wear gloves in case they want to come back. But first we open up the doors and windows."

It took them just a moment to get all the blinds lifted and windows open throughout the place. A bunch of the pictures of naked girls had been taken by the lab techs, but not all of them by a long ways.

"Looks like there are five different girls' pictures on these walls," Cavanaugh said. "The ones in the bedroom on the right seem to be of a girl that isn't here."

Sarge glanced at Pickett and she nodded.

"Let's go out front where it's cooler to talk," Sarge said. "Give this place a chance to cool down."

Cavanaugh in his oversized jacket led the way, going to his car and taking it off and tossing it across the front seat. He had on suspenders holding up his pants and a shoulder holster for his gun and his badge on his belt.

Sarge took off his light jacket that hid his gun and badge as well and Pickett did the same with her jacket, taking them

Don't Miss an Issue!

Subscribe to Smith's Monthly

Electronic or Paper Subscriptions Available.
For Full Subscription Information Go To:

www.SmithsMonthly.com

both to her car and coming back with their bottles of water.

Cavanaugh was still working on his coffee.

"Robin has done her magic again," Pickett said. "She managed to find the real name of this Ben person."

Cavanaugh looked surprised.

They told him how she had done it with facial recognition and high school yearbooks and who his name was.

"And he's still alive," Sarge said, "and supposedly married to Cathy Wendt, the girl that started all this."

Cavanaugh damned near dropped his coffee, which would have been a critical emergency for any detective this early in the morning.

"They are both still alive," Pickett said, "living in a big estate out north of town. Robin doesn't think he knows anything about all of this, even though she has traced the money and buying these homes to him."

Cavanaugh just shook his head. "We got no proof on anyone on this. Except circumstantial with that dead guy in the basement. And we have no idea who he is."

"Think we need some officers sitting on the guy?" Sarge asked.

"Can Robin do that electronically for now?" Cavanaugh asked.

"Let me find out," Pickett said.

She quickly called Robin and asked.

Then Pickett laughed and hung up, smiling. "She's already doing that. She will know when they sleep, flush the toilet, and what they are eating. They won't move without her tracing them. But officially she is not doing that, of course."

"Of course," Cavanaugh said, laughing. "Tell her unofficially thanks. Saved a couple cops some nasty duty for a while."

"I will," Pickett said.

"Embalmed, huh?" Sarge said.

Cavanaugh nodded and finished off his coffee, putting the cup on the roof of his car. "So, ready to see if we can find anything that will help us in that horror house?"

"No," Pickett said.

"We'll just stand out here and cheer you on," Sarge said.

Cavanaugh looked at both of them. "Not damned funny."

"Yes it was," Pickett said, smiling and turning Cavanaugh toward the house and walking with him.

"It was," Sarge said, laughing as he followed them back into a place he really had no desire to ever go again.

FOURTEEN

June 12th, 2017
Las Vegas, Nevada

TWO HOURS LATER the air was starting to heat up and Pickett was covered in dust and sweat. They had carefully looked at every surface through the entire place and found nothing, not even a stray old receipt.

They had moved out into the carport and checked out the car. Pickett stood back and to one side as Cavanaugh popped the trunk. It would not have surprised her that a body was in there, but thankfully just a spare and a jack and nothing under any of it.

There wasn't even anything in the glove box or down under the seats. The car was dirty, but not one detail of who actually had operated it. The owner of record on the books was Ben March. But they had been hoping for more.

As they were standing in the carport, Pickett noticed a wooden ladder leaning against the side of the house under the carport. And that reminded her of one thing they had all forgotten.

"Don't these old homes have small attics?"

Sarge looked at her and Cavanaugh just shook his head.

"I seem to remember an opening in the ceiling of the closet on the left side of the hallway," she said. She had noticed it in the search, but hadn't thought anything about it.

Sarge walked out onto the driveway and studied the roofline. Then he came back nodding. "A person couldn't stand up, but a lot of room up there."

"Ladder is what made me think of it," Pickett said, pointing to the ladder sitting against the wall.

"Last place we check," Sarge said, going over and grabbing the eight-foot tall ladder.

He looked at Cavanaugh. "I'll carry, you climb."

"Just because I am younger than you, right?" Cavanaugh asked as they went back inside and to the bedroom.

"Yeah," Sarge said. "That's it."

When they got to the closet, Pickett pointed out the ladder marks on the wall up high.

"Didn't even notice those," Cavanaugh said, shaking his head. "Maybe I really do need to retire."

"Eighteen more days," Pickett said.

"Who's counting?" Cavanaugh said.

Sarge got the ladder in place and Cavanaugh went up a couple steps, making sure each step was solid, then he pushed open the piece of wood blocking the hole, shoving it to one side.

Sarge handed him a flashlight and Cavanaugh went up two more steps and shined his light around.

Then he said softly, "This can't be happening."

He came down and handed Sarge the flashlight and indicated he should look. "I got some phone calls to make."

He headed out of the bedroom.

Pickett watched him go, then looked back at Sarge. "Do we really want to see what is up there?"

"No," Sarge said. "But after that reaction, I can't not look."

She agreed. She couldn't not look either.

Sarge climbed the ladder in the closet while Pickett held it steady.

Pickett watched from below as Sarge shined the powerful flashlight around.

All Pickett could see was him shaking his head.

Then he came down and handed the flashlight to her. "Not pretty and not something you are going to see every day."

She took the light and went up the ladder, convinced she shouldn't.

She had to go another two steps higher than Sarge or Cavanaugh before she got into the attic enough to see.

It felt hot already up here. She could only imagine how hot it got during the summer days.

There were pieces of plywood covering over the ceiling joists so a person could walk down the middle bent over. She was short enough, she might be able to stand almost upright without banging her head on a roof joist.

But not a chance in hell was she climbing up in there.

She could see the length of the house and on both sides of the middle walkway were bodies stacked on top of one another. All fully dressed, all mummified.

More accurately, baked to a strange, sickly brown color.

And all different ages and races, from what she could tell. Young, old, men, women. All were dressed, at least from the waist up, in dress clothes. At one point they had been in caskets, from the looks of them.

They were stacked like cordwood along both sides. Some face up, some face down into the person below them.

She was numb.

There had to be a hundred bodies up here. And from the looks of it, they had all been here a very, very long time, baking in the summer heat. More than likely for decades.

She had been calling this a house of horrors before now.

The place had now officially earned its name twice over.

She climbed down slowly, handed Sarge the light, and asked, "Can we now get out of this place and never come back?"

"Please," Sarge said.

She led the way down the hall and out the front door.

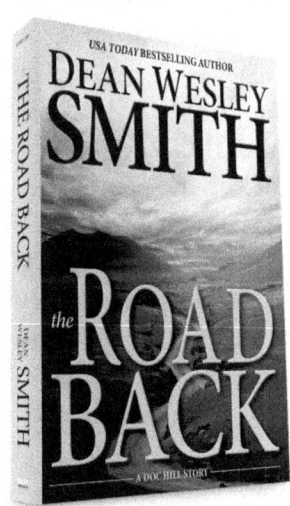

Now Available
from all your favorite booksellers in trade paper and electronic editions.

Cavanaugh was standing beside his car, talking on the phone. She could only imagine the ground-shaking movement this discovery was making in the chief's office.

And there were five more houses that could possibly be just like this one.

This one was bad enough.

And she had a hunch that right now, as of this discovery, the Cold Poker Gang task force was officially off this case. They only dealt with cold cases.

Finding a hundred-plus bodies in one house was now far from cold, even though every person in the house had been dead and roasting in that attic a very long time.

PART THREE
Not Dead Yet

FIFTEEN

June 15th, 2017
Las Vegas, Nevada

FOR THE LAST three days, Sarge had been very relieved that he and Pickett had been off this case and away from those horror houses.

Robin had stayed in contact with Cavanaugh and had kept digging. So this morning at breakfast, she was going to fill them in on what the police had found so far.

And what she had found as well.

The morning air still had a little bite to it, but Sarge had no doubt today was going to be a pretty standard warm June day. Might not hit a hundred, but during the peak time in the afternoon, it might get close.

But now the air was comfortable. The tourists were calm and not many around, so the walk from their condo to the Golden Nugget was easy and enjoyable.

And both of them were curious as to what was going on. Somehow, the entire thing hadn't hit the news yet, which stunned Sarge and Pickett. This should have been a front page, top-of-the-paper story and lead news on every television station. In fact, this should have been on all the national newscasts as well.

Somehow, it wasn't even mentioned and Sarge really wanted to know why. He couldn't believe the department had kept it quiet. No chance of that. Not something this big and with so many people having to be involved with it.

No, the paper and radio stations and television stations were holding this story for some reason and Sarge hoped Robin would know why. And it had to be something larger than hurting tourism, although that reason had gotten a lot of stories downplayed or killed over the years.

They got to the buffet ahead of Robin and since it was his turn to buy, he paid for all three of them while Pickett went ahead to the food. The place smelled so wonderful and rich, with bacon and waffle smells filling the air, he almost didn't want to stop to pay.

He hadn't realized how hungry he really was this morning.

He wasn't far behind her, since the tourist rush was over and there were only about forty people in the large place, most over at tables against the pool windows. No one was sitting near their favorite table.

He had just gotten his omelet and waffle when Robin appeared at the top of the escalator coming up from the casino

to the buffet. He waved her in, signaling she was already paid, and took his food back over to the table.

He and Pickett were half done eating by the time Robin joined them.

For the first ten minutes, as Robin dug into her food, they talked about the three cats and how calm and peaceful the last three days had been for them. They had seen five movies in total, three at night at home and two they had actually gone out to a theater.

"So," Sarge said, stacking his empty plates to one side, "I am dying to know why the media is sitting on this one."

"Families," Robin said. "All those bodies in the attics were supposed to have been cremated thirty and forty years ago."

"Oh, shit," Pickett said.

"Attics?" Sarge asked.

Robin nodded. "All six houses were almost identical. Young blonde girls in beds and buried in the basements, naked pictures on the walls, and bodies stacked in the attics."

Sarge sat back in his chair. He couldn't even think of anything to ask. That was just too much to try to grasp.

"Stunning, isn't it?" Robin said. "I've been trying to get a handle on this for days. Forget all the young girls' bodies in the beds for the moment. The police have to identify and contact well over five hundred families that their grandmother or grandfather or mother or father wasn't really cremated and the ashes they got back were fake. And all from deaths forty years ago."

Sarge just shook his head. "Impossible."

"Matching a body with the right date-of-death is a nightmare all by itself," Robin said. "The media is holding off until they clear out every relative they can find easily, then the media will run with it to try to get the relatives that can't be found and that still care to come out of the woodwork."

"Do they know who did this?"

"No," Robin said. "They know the bodies were supposedly shipped to the county's only crematorium out on the old Boulder Highway from a dozen different mortuaries around town. Back in the early 1970s, pretty much every person who was to be cremated in Las Vegas during those years ended up in the attics of these six houses. Cremation back then was not accepted as much as it is now, so very few opted for it."

"And even though it was only one place, there is still no idea who did this?" Sarge asked. He couldn't believe that was possible.

"Nope," Robin said. "The crematorium was torn down in nineteen-eighty-one so a subdivision could be built, which was pretty much when the last body was put in the attics. That part of the industry was hardly regulated back then in Nevada anyway. And the owner of the crematorium used a fake name."

"Of course," Pickett said.

"They must have made a fortune taking payments for bodies and doing nothing," Sarge said.

He knew that for the longest time, the funeral business was full of scams and fakes. Thankfully, over the last thirty years, new restrictions and rules and organizations had stepped in to keep that sort of thing down to a minimum.

And even though there were five hundred bodies in those attics, the only crime would be fraud and mistreatment of a corpse, both long past statutes of limitations.

This was just a massive PR nightmare.

And all of this had happened before those sorts of government regulations and licensing on the funeral industry came into play. In fact, the years this was happening, the mob and Howard Hughes had just cleared the city and everything was trying to find a new balance.

Sarge just shook his head. "So we have six houses full of bodies. Each house is owned by someone with the fake names of a kid who went to high school as a junior eight years in a row? Right?"

Robin nodded.

"And what about Benjamin Ronald States?" Pickett asked.

"No connection that we can find in the slightest," Robin said. "No one has even gone to talk with him about any of this yet because there is no connection."

"Police a little busy, huh?" Sarge asked, shaking his head.

"Is Cavanaugh going to survive this?" Pickett asked.

"I've talked with him twice a day and he seems to be his normal grumpy self," Robin said. "And the chief has pulled him off of the mortuary problem and has him focused back on the young blondes. They are not mortuary victims, even though they were also embalmed. They are murders."

"How many young girls did it end up being?" Sarge asked, afraid of the answer.

"Thirty-one," Robin said.

"Wow," Pickett said.

"The chief wants us back helping Cavanaugh," Robin said.

Sarge nodded. Part of him was glad to be able to be back on this case. But another part had really liked not thinking about this horror show.

"As long as we don't have to go anywhere near any of those houses," Pickett said.

"I doubt we will," Robin said. "Those are locked down solid and the city is hauling out bodies at night from each home to a few mortuaries who are helping out. They don't want the word out on this either because of the damage it would do to their industry."

"Makes sense," Sarge said. "So any updates on any of the tests on the girls?"

"And the guy in the basement of that first house?" Pickett asked.

Sarge kept forgetting about that guy.

Robin frowned and nodded. "The girls were all killed with blunt force trauma to the back of the head. All with a similar or same weapon."

"So we had a serial killer," Pickett said.

Sarge agreed, especially with the past tense on this. Looked like the killer operated for a short few years and then stopped for some reason.

Or at least Sarge hoped he or she stopped and didn't just move out of town and start up again.

He didn't even want to think of that possibility.

SIXTEEN

June 15th, 2017
Las Vegas, Nevada

ALL THREE OF them had out their notebooks and were trying to figure out what to do next. They had all gotten some more fruit and Sarge had gotten some bacon and they had settled in to work.

All three of them were drinking coffee. Pickett figured it was going to be one of those kind of days when coffee was a very good idea. She hadn't expected the chief to let them back on these cases just yet, but she was glad he had. The regular detectives were just too busy with the mess from all those attics.

"So we forget about the attic stuff," Sarge said. "Let's go over exactly what we do have."

Pickett and Robin both nodded. Pickett figured that if they didn't concentrate down, they would never have even a slight chance of solving this one.

"First," Sarge said, "we have a guy named Ben who came into town, registered as a junior in high school under a fake name, and then did it again for eight straight years, moving from school to school and name to name. Right?"

Robin nodded.

Pickett wrote that down, then put a big "Why" beside the question.

"On another topic, but somehow maybe related," Sarge said, "we have a girl by the name of Cathy Wendt who went missing in June of 1977. She was a junior and her boyfriend's name was Ben. Right?"

"And you traced that Ben from pictures of him in Cathy Wendt's missing person's files to a Benjamin Ronald States, who is still alive and married to Cathy Wendt," Pickett said to Robin.

"Yes," Robin said. "The connection becomes broken when we looked up the old records for a Ben March and he supposedly lived at the house where we found the first bodies. We first thought that Ben March was the same Ben, now we do not know for sure."

"So we have no idea if Ben March is Benjamin States?" Sarge asked a moment before Pickett could.

"That is correct," Robin said. "I have no connection in money or anything else from States to the fake name of March and that house. Or any of the houses."

"Any idea who the guy was in the basement?" Sarge asked.

Robin shook her head. "We should be getting the first rushed DNA tests back on him and those first girls today or tomorrow. Kind of doubt that will help us much unless we get lucky somehow."

Robin looked at some notes, then said, "We do know the old guy in the chair died of dehydration and natural causes. They put his age in the mid-seventies."

Pickett was stunned. "That old? That meant he had to be in his mid-thirties, if not slightly older when those girls were killed."

"Would look that way," Robin said.

Pickett wrote that in her notebook. She had a gut sense that had something to do with all of this, but not a clue what that might be.

All the victims of the murders were about the same age, as best as could be figured without a lot of work. All wore their hair blonde, all were killed in the same fashion, and all were embalmed.

"So on the victims," Pickett said, "our killer had access to a way to embalm his victims."

"Twenty-one official mortuaries in Las Vegas in that time period," Robin said. "Those were the official ones. Embalming was something that could be done by most anyone with the skill and supplies and some basic equipment."

Pickett marked that down and wrote "Dead End" beside it.

"The pictures are another crazy part of this," Sarge said. "How did someone, and for what reason, get those girls to naturally undress for nude pictures?"

"Maybe the promise of being in a major magazine like *Playboy* or *Penthouse* or one of the others men's magazines at the time," Robin said.

Pickett nodded. "That might do it. A promise of money and fame."

"And back then Polaroid pictures were a standard way of doing test shots for major photo shoots," Sarge said, "since the things developed in a minute or so."

"And taking that many of them would be a normal thing for a professional photographer to do," Pickett said. "Could those houses have been used as a form of photography business at one point?"

"I'll look though old newspaper ads and such and see what I can find," Robin said, nodding.

Pickett marked down in her book "Pictures." Then she put a "Possible" beside it.

And that was where they stopped. They seemed to have a lot of information, but all natural ways of looking into all this was blocked by a solid barrier of forty years of time.

So much had changed since the early seventies. Pickett felt like they were living in a different world, the more they looked back through those forty years.

Then it dawned on her that maybe they weren't looking exactly right. They were focused on the eight years and six houses.

She looked up at Sarge, then at Robin. "What happened during the thirty-plus years since all this went on and when that guy died in that basement and the power got turned off to all those houses?"

Sarge just blinked at her.

Robin swore softly and wrote in her notebook.

They needed to start last year, with modern techniques, and trace backwards. And Pickett knew exactly where to start.

"The cars," Pickett said. "We start with the cars and work backwards. There have to be cameras and other records in car lots and at the Department of Motor Vehicles."

Both Sarge and Robin nodded and both kept writing in their notebooks, which was a very good sign.

SEVENTEEN

June 15th, 2017
Las Vegas, Nevada

SARGE REALLY LIKED the idea that they start with the cars. Turns out each house had a car parked in the driveway. And all were as clean as the one they had first looked at. It made no sense, but Pickett was right, it was a way to bring this investigation to now and work backwards.

And there was another way, but Sarge figured it was a long shot.

"How about we go talk with Benjamin States," he said.

"Think Cavanaugh could get that approved at this point?"

Robin shrugged. "Let me find out."

She took her phone out of her bag and hit a number and put the phone to her ear. "Cavanaugh," she said. "Got the gang here finishing breakfast and getting ready to go to work."

She listened for a moment, then nodded. "We're wondering if you could arrange for us, with you along if you have time, to go talk with Benjamin States and his wife."

She listened, then laughed. "Fire me the address. Sarge and Pickett will meet

you there. I've got some tracing to do on those six cars we found."

She listened for a moment, then said "Thanks," and hung up.

"He already got it approved and figured we would ask, so he called the couple and set up an appointment in one hour at their home."

Pickett laughed and Sarge just shook his head.

"Cavanaugh is going to be a great addition to this task force," Sarge said.

"If the paperwork on this case doesn't kill him first," Pickett said, and they all laughed.

Fifty-five minutes later, after a brisk walk back to the condo to get the car and some ice in an ice chest and bottles of water, they made it to Benjamin States' gated home on a sprawling acreage overlooking the Las Vegas valley.

"Wow," Pickett said as they drove slowly up the twisting drive through the rocks and desert plants toward the big white stucco mansion that seemed to spread over the top of the rock bluff.

Sarge could only agree. It was an impressive place.

And expensive. Millions and millions expensive.

They pulled up and stopped in front of the home on a massive circular driveway. Pickett left the car running to keep the air-conditioning going and they both got a bottle of water from the cooler.

They didn't dare make a move until Cavanaugh was with them. This was still an active case after all and they needed an active detective.

It seemed very strange to be working a live case again. Very strange.

A few moments later Cavanaugh pulled in behind them.

He met them beside Pickett's Jeep and indicated the house. "You two are rich, why don't you live in a place like this?"

"We're not that rich," Pickett said.

"And we can't walk to breakfast either," Sarge said, pointing back toward the city in the distance. This place was beautiful, but it was a way out of town.

"Yeah, good point there," Cavanaugh said. "I'll let you off the hook this time."

"Thanks," Pickett said, laughing. "You getting any sleep?"

"Like a log for four hours a night. Two naps a day when I can catch them. I plan on getting old enough to join you guys in the Gang."

"Fifteen days," Pickett said.

"Oh, really, I had lost track," Cavanaugh said, then laughed.

The three of them turned to the massive ornate wood front door of the big mansion. The door was so huge, it either had to be balanced perfectly or it would need a machine to open it. Sarge figured it to be almost two stories tall.

Turned out, after they knocked, it opened easily in perfect balance to show an even larger and more ornate stone and tile and rough wood room beyond.

The man that met them was medium height, wearing tan slacks, a light shirt, and slippers. He had his gray hair cut short and had striking blue eyes. He looked to be in his fifties or early sixties and was clearly in great shape.

He introduced himself as Benjamin States, but that they could call him Ben. They shook his hand and gave their names and showed their badges. He then asked them to come in.

He led them through the massive tile-floored and high-ceilinged front foyer with a staircase that looked like it might go on forever upward. They ended the

trip in what looked to be a library, with maple shelving and walls full of expensive leather books.

The place had a wonderful warm feel, which surprised Sarge considering the rest of the house had felt cold. And the room smelled a little of the remains of breakfast, so the kitchen must be close by as well.

There was a rock fireplace filling one wall with a large television hung over the mantel and two comfortable recliners facing it.

Two couches framed the seating area with a large wooden coffee table in the center, covered mostly in magazines.

At that moment an older woman with short gray hair and a bright smile came into the room. She seemed to also be in great shape.

Her husband did the introductions, introducing her as his wife, Cathy.

They all took a seat, Sarge and Pickett on one couch, Cavanaugh on the other, and the two States in their respective reading chairs.

Now Available
from all your favorite booksellers in trade paper and electronic editions.

"So, detectives, what can we do to help you?" Ben asked.

"Well," Cavanaugh said, sitting forward. "We have a real mess on our hands and we don't even know where to start. So let me have Pickett and Sarge here tell you how they got all this started and how your names got into the investigation."

Both Cathy and Ben frowned, but nodded.

"Pickett and I are members of a cold case special task force," Sarge said. "We were handed the very cold case of a missing girl by the name of Cathy Wendt."

Sarge was watching Cathy's reaction and she instantly had one, sitting back and then looking at Ben.

"We had very little to go on," Pickett said, "considering that was forty years ago. So we talked to the brother who was of no help, then we went to Cathy Wendt's old boyfriend's home."

Sarge watched as Ben nodded on that.

"The power had been turned off for about a year and inside we found a number of things," Sarge said. "First, we found a man sitting in a rocking chair in the basement, staring at the graves of three young girls. He had dug up one of them a little."

"Oh, my," Cathy said, covering her mouth.

"We thought at first that one of them was Cathy Wendt and her boyfriend, Ben March, had killed her," Pickett said. "But it turns out there was another mummified body of a young girl with blonde hair in a bed upstairs. All of the four of them had been dead for a very long time, more than likely since the seventies. We have yet to identify any of them."

Sarge was watching Ben and Cathy and they seemed seriously stunned and shocked. A normal reaction to hearing something like that.

"Here is where things get even stranger," Sarge said, skipping the part about bodies in the attic for now. "There was a picture of Cathy and Ben in the missing person's file. We ran a facial recognition scan on Ben's face and found that he was really Benjamin Ronald States, twenty-three at the time, who moved to Las Vegas in 1975."

"And we know that you are Cathy Wendt, our missing person from 1977," Pickett said to Cathy.

Cathy nodded and looked to her husband, who only nodded.

"Ben got me away from my father and mother," Cathy said. "I was sixteen and of age for the time in Las Vegas, so we did nothing illegal. But I knew that if I didn't vanish, my parents would not let me leave. In fact, I was certain they would kill me if I tried. To say the least, I came from a very abusive family."

"So we left town for six months," Ben said, "living in Washington state and in Canada for most of it. Then we came back."

"I dyed my hair brown," Cathy said, "always wore sunglasses when I went out

USA TODAY BESTSELLING AUTHOR
DEAN WESLEY SMITH
AN EASY SHOT
A GOLF THRILLER

Now Available
from all your favorite booksellers
in trade paper and electronic editions.

for years, and we managed to avoid my parents and brother and friends. No one knew until now."

"So you were Ben March?" Sarge asked.

Ben nodded. "I assume you know if you traced when I got out here that I changed my name and enrolled as a junior every year for eight years in different schools. I met Cathy on the third year of doing that and we have been together ever since."

"And you had that three-bedroom house under your Ben March name?"

"I did," Ben said, nodding. "When we left town I put it on the market and it sold within a month or so. I have no idea what happened to it. I never checked."

Cavanaugh looked at his notebook and then asked Ben about the other five homes.

Ben nodded with each. "I owned them all for one year each, paid cash for them, sold them at a slight profit after a year."

"We would fix them up some," Cathy said. "New paint, new carpet, make a little profit. It was fun for me to help with as I was going to college."

"The records we could find show that you still own all those homes," Sarge said. "Under your different names."

"Not a chance," Ben said, now clearly upset. "I was paid for those homes by my broker. Never had another thing to do with them."

"We know that," Pickett said.

Cavanaugh nodded and Ben seemed to relax some.

"We know that somehow the records were falsified," Sarge said, "to leave your fake name on the home, but we can't figure out why just yet."

"So if you don't mind my asking," Pickett said, "why did you buy those homes and sign up as a junior in different schools every year?"

"To meet girls," Ben said, then he smiled at Cathy.

Cathy nodded. "He's telling you the truth. Ben is a world-famous photographer of nudes. His work hangs all over the world in galleries."

"We know that as well," Cavanaugh said, nodding.

"So with him as a junior and me as his girlfriend from another school, he could meet girls who wanted to do some modeling. We used the homes to not only fix up to sell, but for a studio."

"Magazine work?" Pickett asked.

"Some at first," Ben said. "But the magazines of that time were turning more toward porn than erotica and I stopped. It was in about that time period that we started our company and the photography went from the main focus to a background work."

"Now it is back as the main focus," Cathy said.

Sarge looked at her. She was clearly very proud of her husband's work.

"Did you take Polaroid pictures of the models to start with?" Pickett asked.

"I did," Ben said.

"What happened to all those pictures?" Sarge asked.

"They were destroyed in 1981 when the building that I leased a small office and darkroom from burnt down."

"Luckily we had most of the negatives of his important photos and all the records at home," Cathy said.

Sarge just nodded. Now they at least understood a little more of what had happened. Clearly these two had had a stalker back then who not only followed them, but killed some of his models, stole those pictures, and burnt down his darkroom.

"Did the model releases survive the fire?" Pickett asked.

"They did," Ben said. "They were also at home."

Sarge looked at Picket and then at Cavanaugh. It seemed that maybe, just maybe, they had caught a break.

EIGHTEEN

June 15th, 2017
Las Vegas, Nevada

BEN AND CATHY asked the three of them to join them in the kitchen.

"Sorry for my manners," Cathy said. "I should have offered you all a drink."

"Oh, we're fine, ma'am," Cavanaugh said, smiling his best and most friendly smile.

The kitchen was state of the art, as Pickett would have expected, but also very comfortable. Rough, natural-colored wooden beams ran across the ceiling and old-style pendant lights hung down over a massive island covered in quartz.

Three skylights in the high ceiling also let in natural light.

The place had a wonderful faint odor of bacon, more than likely cooked for breakfast.

Cathy got all three of the detectives a glass of ice water, Ben a glass of iced tea, and herself a glass of some sort of juice with ice.

"So I am assuming that since you mentioned my model releases, you would like to see them?" Ben asked.

"If we could," Cavanaugh said. "We will, of course, keep all information in them completely private."

"Why?" Ben asked. "I have a feeling there is something you are not telling us."

"We believe the girls found dead in that house might have been your models," Pickett said.

Both Ben and Cathy looked puzzled. Both shook their heads.

Pickett was absolutely sure that they had nothing to do with this. They didn't seem to be covering anything up. But there was just no telling.

Sarge looked at Cavanaugh and he nodded, so Sarge turned to Ben. "The Polaroid pictures you took were on the walls of the houses. Thousands of them total in each house."

Cathy and Ben looked like they were going to be sick.

"How is that possible?" Cathy asked.

"We'll investigate the fire to your darkroom and office building," Pickett said. "But just guessing, someone broke in there, stole them all, and set the place on fire."

"Would they have also gotten the names of the models from records there?" Sarge asked.

Ben nodded slowly.

"I think I'm going to be sick," Cathy said.

Ben reached over and touched her hand, which seemed to calm her some. Clearly these two had been in love for a very long time. And were still good for each other.

"How many girls?" Ben asked after a long moment of silence in the big kitchen.

Pickett glanced at Cavanaugh, who shook his head slightly. Clearly he wanted to keep the number secret.

"We honestly don't know yet," Pickett said, "because there is another factor clogging up the investigation and making it much worse."

"Worse than this?" Cathy asked, her voice a little shrill.

"We need you to promise for a time to keep what we are about to tell you to yourselves completely," Cavanaugh said.

Both nodded.

"Each house had a small attic," Sarge said.

Both Ben and Cathy nodded.

"The attics were full of bodies that should have been cremated, but were not."

"Full?" Ben asked.

Sarge nodded.

"Right now the police and the press are keeping a lid on this until families can be notified. But it seems for about six years or so, all the bodies in the entire Las Vegas area that were to be cremated instead ended up stored in the attics of those homes."

"Oh, god, no," Cathy said, covering her mouth and turning and running from the room.

Ben watched her go. He had his back to the detectives.

Then he seemed to gather himself together and turned back to them. "Were all the victims blonde? Like Cathy used to be?"

"Yes," Cavanaugh said. "And Polaroid pictures of Cathy were on one wall. In a room without a body."

"Were all the bodies embalmed?" Ben asked.

Now it was Sarge and Pickett and Cavanaugh's turn to be shocked.

Pickett was surprised that either this guy was admitting he did it, or if he had, he was really stunningly good at acting.

"Yes, they were," Cavanaugh said. "But no one knows that either. How did you guess that?"

"The monster that was Cathy's father embalmed bodies for a living," Ben said.

"The son-of-a-bitch clearly must have always known where we were."

Pickett just stared at Sarge.

And silence hung over the room until Cavanaugh took out his phone and called the lab.

"DNA results in on the old man in the basement?"

Pickett watched as Cavanaugh listened.

"Compare the old man against the DNA sample from Cathy Wendt's brother. Get back to me as quickly as you can."

He hung up.

Ben was nodding and looking troubled.

Then Ben said, "Excuse me, I need to go see how Cathy is doing. We will be right back."

As Ben left, Pickett took out her phone and called Robin. They had their first real lead on all of this, and if it panned out, might answer a ton of questions.

If it panned out.

And honestly, Pickett felt like it just might.

And that worried her.

NINETEEN

June 15th, 2017
Las Vegas, Nevada

SARGE WATCHED AS Ben brought Cathy back into the warm and comfortable kitchen and had her sit at the counter and sip on her juice.

"I'm sorry for my reaction," Cathy said after a moment.

"Completely understandable," Pickett said. "We came in here and blindsided you with all this stuff from the ancient past."

Cathy nodded. "I was in counseling for over ten years because of what that monster of a father did to me. Ben rescued me from my father and mother."

Sarge watched, as did Cavanaugh and Pickett. Sarge had a hunch that if anyone could talk to Cathy, it would be Pickett.

"So your father was an undertaker?" Pickett asked.

"No," Cathy said. "Just an embalmer. But he loved dead bodies. He used to make Mom and I lay naked on the kitchen table and pretend we were dead."

"Your mother helped with his sickness?" Pickett asked.

Sarge could tell that Pickett was now really shocked, even though he knew she shouldn't be. Mothers often helped facilitate child abuse by simply pretending it never happened. Pickett knew that.

Sometimes it was because the wives feared the husband, sometimes because back fifty years or more ago, the women looked away because they didn't think it was wrong. Fathers owned the wife and the children and could do what they wanted with them.

Things had really changed for the better in that area.

Cathy nodded. "My mother was a beaten, controlled, mind-dead woman by the time I left. She helped the monster and never protected me. Then refused to talk with me about it, as if it never happened. I actually think she enjoyed it, to be honest."

Sarge felt like he wanted to be sick now. No matter how long on the force you dealt with the sick and perverted of humanity, a person never got used to it. Especially when it came to what adults did to children.

Cavanaugh was just staring down at the pattern in the quartz countertop, not moving.

"So you think your father might have discovered what you and Ben were doing after you vanished?" Pickett asked.

"We saw no evidence of that until you brought this here now," Ben said. "But embalming the girls and the bodies in the attic make sense for it to be him. He was that sick. And I am sure he wanted to get back at me for taking Cathy from him."

Sarge nodded. It did make sense. That would explain leaving Ben's fake name on the houses.

"Why didn't he just report you?" Pickett asked.

"Because he knew that if he did I would tell the world what he was doing to me and my mother," Cathy said, coldness in her voice. "And I would have, too."

Ben nodded to that. "We considered turning him in a number of times. But it was the 1970s and times were very different then. Things were only starting to change, but parents still had the say over the kids and could do what they wanted with them. Everyone, including the police, just looked the other way."

Sarge remembered that well from his early days on the force.

"Any idea how he might have gotten to all those bodies stashed in the attic?" Cavanaugh asked.

Both Cathy and Ben shook their heads.

"We paid no attention to him as we tried to build our lives," Ben said.

At that point Cavanaugh's phone buzzed and he looked at it and then said, "Excuse me for a moment."

He clicked on the phone and said, "Yeah."

He listened, then said, "Thank you."

He hung up and looked directly at Cathy and Ben. "You no longer ever have to worry about that man. It was his body we found in the basement of the March house. They matched his DNA to your brother."

Cathy just shook her head.

Ben looked sick.

"That's not good news?" Pickett asked.

Cathy shook her head and clearly couldn't speak.

Finally Ben said, "Her brother had a different father."

"Oh," Pickett said. "Do you know that man's name?"

Cathy and Ben both shook their heads no.

"My mom told me once, in private, that I should never tell my father. She said she had gotten tired of my father's perverted games and wanted real sex, so she met a guy and got pregnant. She never told me who that was."

"Oh," Pickett said again.

All Sarge could do was the same thing Cavanaugh was doing, stare at the pattern in the quartz countertop in front of him.

TWENTY

June 15th, 2017
Las Vegas, Nevada

PICKETT DIDN'T KNOW what to think at this point.

Cathy, looking very pale, finally asked to be excused to go lie down.

Ben walked her out of the room after telling Cavanaugh he would be back with the model records and releases after he got Cathy resting.

Pickett glanced at Sarge, then at Cavanaugh, when it was only the three of them in the kitchen. "I think they are telling the truth," she said, her voice low.

Cavanaugh nodded.

So did Sarge.

"So Cathy's brother's father is the dead guy in the basement," Sarge said. "But we still don't know who he was."

"Maybe the brother will tell us if he knows," Cavanaugh said.

"Cathy knew her father had a sexual thing for dead women," Pickett said. "Any chance there is any way of knowing if those women were sexually abused after they were killed?"

Cavanaugh shrugged at that. "Mummy sex? I suppose in Las Vegas anything is possible."

Pickett tried not to laugh as Cavanaugh took out his phone and called a number with one button. After a moment he said, "Cavanaugh again. Got another question for you on the blonde girl victims from the houses. Any chance you can tell if their bodies were sexually abused."

He listened for a minute, then his eyes got wide and he just sat there, listening and shaking his head.

Pickett was completely sure that if the news got to Cavanaugh like that, she wasn't going to want to hear it.

Finally Cavanaugh said, "Could you send that report to Robin on the Cold Case Task Force, please."

He nodded, then said, "Thank you."

He clicked off his phone and glanced around to make sure that Ben wasn't coming back into the room.

Then he leaned forward and said softly, "The four girls in the first house were all embalmed. All had their private parts sewn open so that they would be easy to have sex with after they were dead."

"Now I want to be sick," Pickett said.

Sarge just shook his head. This case was going beyond disgusting and right down into totally unthinkable.

"It gets worse," Cavanaugh said.

"How can that get worse?" Sarge asked.

Pickett wanted to ask the same question. How could it be worse than that?

Cavanaugh looked around to make sure Ben hadn't returned then he said simply, "The girl's body under the sheet was dressed in a sheer nightgown and there are signs of at least five or six different DNA semen samples in the body in the bed, plus lubricant. Some of it seemingly fresh. They are working to try to get DNA."

Sarge glanced at Pickett who was as pale as Cathy had looked a moment ago.

He took a deep breath and took a large drink of the water in front of him.

Pickett did the same.

"And it goes on," Cavanaugh said, after also taking a drink.

"I am pretty sure I don't want to know what 'goes on' means," Pickett said.

Sarge nodded.

Cavanaugh looked around again, then once again leaned forward. "The body half dug-up in the basement with the hair and the hand showing?"

Now Available
from all your favorite booksellers
in trade paper and electronic editions.

DEATH TAKES A PARTNER
A MARY JO ASSASSIN NOVEL

DEAN WESLEY SMITH
USA TODAY BESTSELLING AUTHOR

"Don't tell me," Sarge sat back.

Pickett wanted to just cover her ears.

Cavanaugh nodded. "Semen all over the hand and in the hair from numbers of men."

There was not a thing any of them could say to that.

Three hardened, Las Vegas career detectives, shocked to their cores.

TWENTY-ONE

June 15th, 2017
Las Vegas, Nevada

PICKETT WAS SIPPING on the ice water, trying to clear her mind, when Ben returned carrying an old file box that looked dusty and had clearly seen the wear of years.

"Sorry about the dust on this stuff," he said. "Been saving it to donate to some university collection somewhere, after I die. Cathy's idea."

He set the box on the counter and opened the lid, showing neat rows of files, all labeled by the year.

"I photographed only about six or seven girls a year from the year I arrived here until Cathy and I turned our attention to our business and I dropped the photography for a while."

Pickett could see that he had kept good records and she was surprised they had survived so long. But it made sense considering how well known he was for his art.

"Can we look at the March house files," Cavanaugh said. "Once you and Cathy were together?"

Ben nodded and pulled out 1977. "It was Cathy and her natural blonde hair that got me interested in blondes and a book came out of it that started to make my reputation as an artist, actually. Although I didn't take advantage of it until almost a decade later."

He handed Cavanaugh the file and left the room, coming back a moment later with a large photo book of nudes. The title was just *Blondes.* He handed that to Pickett.

"Some of the women, if I remember right, from the 1977 March house are in that book," Ben said.

Pickett opened the book. It was heavy and very well done. The copyright was 1981. The book's dedication was "To my beautiful wife Cathy."

Pickett was impressed. All the women were blonde, all the photos were art photos, very well done, very tastefully posed.

And about half of the backgrounds were regular bedrooms like the ones in those horror homes.

Pickett leafed through it, then handed it to Sarge, who did the same.

"So these are the names and addresses of the six women you photographed that year in the March house. Correct?" Cavanaugh asked.

Ben glanced at the folder that Cavanaugh had, then said, "Yes, that is correct."

"Would you mind if I give these names to another detective?" Cavanaugh asked. "Again, we will do our best to keep these completely confidential."

"If it helps with this, please," Ben said.

Pickett watched as Sarge called Robin, then clicked pictures of the files and sent them to her. Then he hung up.

Knowing Robin, they would know more about those girls very shortly.

Pickett watched as Cavanaugh took out the 1978 file and looked at it.

"Anything more you can tell us about Cathy's family?" Pickett asked of Ben. "Her father, brother, anything that might help us on this?"

"Her father was one sick son-of-a-bitch," Ben said, clear coldness in his voice. "I only met him twice and didn't like him. When Cathy first told me what he was doing to her and her mother, I wanted to go kill him. Cathy made me not do that."

"Smart woman," Sarge said.

Ben just nodded. Pickett could tell that Ben wasn't convinced that was the right decision yet.

"Did she know who you actually were by that point?" Pickett asked.

"Yes," Ben said. "The moment we started falling in love, I told her the complete truth. And that was when I started learning about her father as well."

"And you never thought to check on him after you two left?" Sarge asked.

"Never," Ben said. "Cathy and I thought we had escaped. Our focus was to put that behind us. Cathy only felt bad about leaving her little brother in there, but we had no real choice. He was only five and she knew her father and mother had no interest in boys at all. Only girls in their sick games around death. So we figured he would be all right. Another reason to not look and check on what they were doing. We just didn't want to know."

Pickett understood that. She hadn't really checked on her ex-husband who left her for an overblown chest because she just didn't want to know.

Cavanaugh's phone buzzed and he answered it with a "Yes."

Pickett watched as he listened for a moment. She knew he was talking with Robin. She had no idea how much of what Robin was telling him he would decide to share with Ben.

And since this was Cavanaugh's case, that was his decision.

After a moment Cavanaugh said, "I will check."

Cavanaugh turned to Ben. "May I send the names for the next six or seven years as well? It is going to take some time to research all these since so many years have passed and we don't want to bother you and Cathy again if we can help it."

Pickett nodded to Sarge. Cavanaugh was very slick. He had decided to not tell Ben anything more.

Ben said, "Sure, go ahead."

He opened up the files for Cavanaugh.

"Photos of the other years coming through now," Cavanaugh said.

Then with Ben helping, Cavanaugh took a photo of each page with the girls' names and information and model releases and sent it to Robin.

They got to 1982 and Ben said, "The blonde project was over by this point and I only did one shoot. And none for the next four years after that."

Cavanaugh nodded, took the one last picture of the records from 1982, checked with Robin that she got them all, then hung up.

"Thank you," Cavanaugh said, reaching out to Ben and shaking his hand as he stood. "And apologize to Cathy for us for upsetting her."

Pickett and Sarge followed Cavanaugh's lead, thanking Ben and heading toward the front door.

Cavanaugh handed Ben a card. "Please, if you can think of anything more you might know, call me at any point."

"We will," Ben said. "I am sure this will be a topic of conversation for us for the first time in a decade."

"I am sorry about that," Cavanaugh said.

"Detectives, please don't be sorry," Ben said. "You are only doing your jobs."

Five minutes later Pickett had then headed down the long driveway from the beautiful home. They were headed for lunch at the Bellagio Café. Cavanaugh was following them in his car.

It seems they had made progress.

And slid backward at the same time.

Robin was going to meet them for lunch, and Pickett had a hunch Robin knew who the victims were now.

And as sad as that was, it actually was progress.

But they still didn't know who the killer was or what was actually going on in those six houses of horror.

TWENTY-TWO

June 15th, 2017
Las Vegas, Nevada

SARGE AND PICKETT got to the Bellagio Café before both Robin and Cavanaugh. They managed to get a waiter to clear off their favorite booth from a group that had it before them. The sounds of the casino felt normal and the smell of the food calmed Sarge. The conversation this morning was anything but calming, that was for sure.

As they got seated, Cavanaugh joined them.

Sarge watched the detective sort of slow-walk his way toward the table through the crowded restaurant. Cavanaugh was an amazing man and an amazing detective. The regular force was going to miss him, but the Cold Poker Gang were all going to welcome him with open arms.

"Well, this is a sick mess," Cavanaugh said as he slid into the booth.

"They didn't clean off your side of the table there or something?" Pickett asked, pretending to be serious.

Cavanaugh actually snorted.

"Thank you," he said, winking at her. "I needed that."

Pickett and Sarge had talked about the case on the way into town. The fact that the houses actually had regular visitors just recently might just help them. More than likely that sort of thing was set up over the dark web, but Robin and her people were really good at tracing damn near anything.

"The depravity of the human animal, especially in this town, never ceases to amaze me," Sarge said.

"As old and jaded as we are as detectives," Pickett said, "you think we would be used to anything."

"Speak for yourself about the old part," Cavanaugh said, smiling at her. "I have fifteen days before I become officially old."

"Noted," Pickett said, smiling.

"So what did you two think of old Ben and Cathy?" Cavanaugh asked.

"I think Cathy was an abuse victim," Pickett said. "Seen a lot of that over the years and she sure didn't seem to be faking any of those reactions, although I could be wrong on that."

"Agreed," Sarge said. "And Ben seems to be, on the surface, a really good guy who rescued the woman he loved. And they have been a team ever since."

Sarge worried about that reaction. It wasn't normal for him to have a suspect he completely believed. It had happened, but rarely. It happened again today with Ben and Cathy.

"Think it a little weird that Cathy helped him with his nude photography?" Cavanaugh asked. "After all that happened with her and her father and mother?"

"No," Pickett said, shaking her head. "The photography wasn't about sex, it was about fun and art. Remember how happy all those women in those pictures were? Cathy made being naked natural and fun and alive for the woman, not something twisted and ugly and dead like her father had done."

Cavanaugh nodded.

"So Robin knew who some of the victims are?" Sarge asked.

"Yup," Cavanaugh said. "No point in telling Ben about the other stuff, especially about what happened to his models because he photographed them. With luck, he will never learn that part. Bad enough they were killed because he and Cathy had photographed them."

Sarge agreed. It was going to be hard enough when Ben completely realized that someone targeted the women he found, the ones he put in his book, and then had killed them. Ben and Cathy didn't need the rest of it.

Now Available
from all your favorite booksellers in trade paper and electronic editions.

DEATH TAKES A DIAMOND

A MARY JO ASSASSIN NOVEL

DEAN WESLEY SMITH

USA TODAY BESTSELLING AUTHOR

"Are we missing something here?" Sarge asked, suddenly realizing that he had looked at a book full of nudes from a professional photographer. "There are a lot of nut jobs out there who might hate what Ben was doing with the nudes."

"Some religious zealot who thinks nudity is a sin and the sinner should be punished?" Cavanaugh asked, nodding. "Maybe."

"We could even have a sick boyfriend of one of the girls be our killer," Pickett said.

"So our suspect pool just grew," Cavanaugh said, shaking his head. "Wonderful, just wonderful."

Sarge felt exactly the same way. They needed to narrow the suspects, not increase them.

TWENTY-THREE

June 15th, 2017
Las Vegas, Nevada

PICKETT WATCHED AS Robin wound her way through the tables of the Bellagio Café toward them. She had a backpack over her shoulder which meant she was carrying a lot of information and her computer.

Robin joined them. "Ain't this case a pile of joy?"

"Sick doesn't even start to describe it," Pickett said.

Everyone nodded.

"So do we now know who all the victims are?" Sarge asked.

"All but three of the thirty-one," Robin said. "They didn't disappear the year that States did his photography shoot. In fact, they all disappeared in 1981 and were killed and embalmed that year."

"After the fire at his dark room office," Pickett said.

Robin nodded. "It was a pretty extreme missing person's year that year and had a police task force set up on the cases, but without luck."

"Eighty-one was the last year Ben owned one of those houses, right?" Cavanaugh asked.

"Yes," Robin said. "And the last year the crematorium existed out off the old highway."

"So the timeline all fits," Pickett said. "If we can assume that Cathy's father was doing this, he was trying to destroy Ben and Cathy by putting all the bodies up in the attics in homes they owned."

"Looks that way," Robin said. "At least that's one theory. I have no other at the moment, to be honest."

Pickett had her notebook open and went to a couple questions she had.

"How did Cathy's father manage to keep Ben's fake name on the title when he bought it?"

"I don't know yet," Robin said.

Now Available
from all your favorite booksellers in trade paper and electronic editions.

USA TODAY BESTSELLING AUTHOR
DEAN WESLEY SMITH
STARBURST
A SEEDERS UNIVERSE NOVEL

"He just had a fake broker send fake paperwork to Ben," Cavanaugh said, "and the money and have him sign. The house never really transferred, although Ben thought it did and got paid for it."

Pickett looked at Cavanaugh and the detective shrugged. "Worked a scam case back about fifteen years ago where that was the scam. Only the buyers were getting drug houses to use, leaving the original owners holding the bag."

Sarge shook his head. "A great way to get storage. The guy putting the bodies up in the attic was getting the money for the houses from the bodies."

"How much were they paying the crematorium for each cremation?"

"Nine hundred a body," Robin said. "Some more, but nine hundred was the minimum at that time."

"For a hundred bodies a house," Sarge said, "that's ninety grand. Wow. What did that house sell for back then?"

"Twenty-three thousand," Robin said, glancing at her notes.

Pickett was stunned. The money explained a lot of this.

At that moment the waiter came to take their order.

They all four ordered lunches and iced teas, then after the waiter left, Robin said, "Want the real disgusting stuff now?"

Pickett shook her head no.

"Do we have to?" Sarge asked.

"Getting old is making these two whiners, isn't it?" Cavanaugh asked Robin.

"No," Robin said, smiling, "they just know when I say something is disgusting, it is really disgusting."

"Now I don't want to hear it either," Cavanaugh said.

"Too late," Pickett said, laughing. "She's going to tell us anyway."

Robin nodded and dug out some notes.

"I called a friend at the lab who was working on this case and she and I decided to focus in on just one body in the second house that was in the bed upstairs."

Pickett nodded. "I told you about how the body was embalmed with the genitals sewn open? From what my friend can tell, the body was 'cleaned out' every few months or so for the entire thirty-five years since the poor woman was killed and embalmed."

"Oh, my god," Cavanaugh said, shaking his head.

"So we only have DNA traces for the last five or six uses of the corpse."

"Five or six uses in three months?"

Robin nodded. "That was just one body."

"So why did they bury some of the girls," Sarge asked, "if they were being used?"

"Burying didn't stop the use," Robin said. "Each basement had a shovel in it and each body had been buried in a very shallow grave in a black tarp that the forensics are getting prints off of. A lot of prints. Seems the girls were being dug up and reburied all the time."

Pickett just sort of shuddered. This really was disgusting. Robin had been right.

"Are you telling me that a guy could go in there, dig up a girl and have sex with her?" Cavanaugh asked.

Robin nodded. "I found the listings for the houses on the dark web. The listings have not been updated and are not responding. But yes, exactly that."

"Any way to trace those listings?"

"Will has his best working on it," Robin said. "Trying to come at it from the contact side. But looks as if the clientele of these houses were from all over the world. And they paid $5,000 for two days' rental of the house. Unlimited use of the facilities."

Pickett just shook her head and tried not to imagine any of it.

Sarge looked at the stunned face of Cavanaugh. "I warned you about when Robin says something is disgusting, don't ask."

Cavanaugh laughed. "That's some pretty sick shit."

"Very sick," Pickett said. "Very damned sick."

TWENTY-FOUR

June 15th, 2017
Las Vegas, Nevada

THEY ATE THEIR lunches and talked about other things beside the case, which Sarge was very happy to do at this point. This case was not one that made eating easy, and he had eaten at some pretty nasty crime scenes.

But something about abusing the corpse of a young woman for thirty-five years just made him sick and want to punch someone. Any of the sick bastards who used those houses would do.

Sarge hoped that the families of all those girls would never know what their daughter's body had ever gone through after death. Just no point at all in telling them.

After they got done with lunch and were just talking, the conversation came back to the case.

"So we are going to close thirty-one missing person's cold cases," Pickett said.

"Thirty-two," Robin said, "counting Cathy and Ben."

"Forgot about that one," Pickett said. "The one that started all this."

"So how do we figure out who Cathy's brother's father was, the guy in that basement?" Sarge asked. "The brother flat didn't want to cooperate much at all when we talked to him about Cathy."

Cavanaugh shrugged. "How about we go see him and I threaten to take him downtown and question him for murder if he doesn't talk."

Sarge laughed. "He was only nine or ten in 1981."

"We won't tell him which murders," Cavanaugh said. "And we can get him if he withholds information as well if we want."

"Can't hurt," Pickett said and Sarge agreed.

"I'm headed back to see if Will and his people have managed any forward motion from the computer side and then help on the scanning of fingerprints from the tarps and shovels and other places in those houses. If we find one of the creeps and threaten to expose him, he might roll on the people who ran the operation."

Sarge really liked that idea.

"I want to be the one to question the guy," Cavanaugh said, "preferably in a dark alley with a dumpster nearby."

Pickett laughed. Then raised her hand. "Can I help?"

"I am going to be so happy when you join the gang," Sarge said to Cavanaugh.

Robin nodded as she gathered up her stuff and put it back in her pack. "You certainly fit with this bunch, that's for sure."

Cavanaugh only shrugged. "Fifteen days. And then someone else gets to do the rest of the paperwork on this mess."

Cavanaugh decided to leave his car at the Bellagio and ride with Pickett and Sarge out the Strip to where Kevin Wendt worked. They knew he was on duty, so they were just going to surprise him.

They found Kevin just as he was coming off his shift, and Cavanaugh flashed his badge and said they needed to talk.

Kevin was a short guy, not more than five-three, and wore lift boots to make him seem a little taller. He had dark black hair, dark eyes, and a chin that didn't seem to exist at times. He wore the standard dealer's blue shirt, dark vest, and dark slacks.

From what Robin had found out about him, he had been married once and divorced and lived in an apartment within walking distance of his job. He had been dealing blackjack now for eleven years and had a clean reputation at work.

He had no debts, but few bills, and didn't seem to spend much money at all. He seemed to be just surviving, which was the opinion Sarge had left with when they talked with him the first time.

Angry surviving, but surviving.

They showed their badges and got off the casino floor and back into a meeting room.

"Still looking for my long-dead sister?" Kevin asked as he dropped down into a chair and let the others take a seat around the Formica table.

There was a projector screen on one wall at the end of the table and a dozen chairs around the table. Some work posters covered another wall. Otherwise this was just a regular, plain meeting room like Sarge had seen a hundred times over the years, plain, dull, without a window and only one wooden door.

"Her case has expanded some," Cavanaugh said. "And we think your father is involved."

"That sick bastard vanished in 1981 when I was twelve and mom had become useless to his sex games."

Sarge was stunned that Kevin knew about those and admitted it. That did not bode well.

"Not that father," Cavanaugh said. "Your biological father."

Kevin did not react as Sarge had expected him to act. Instead Kevin's eyes got cold and he said, "How did you know about him?"

"DNA," Cavanaugh said. "We found his body at the scene of a pretty major crime. And we think you might be involved as well."

Kevin sat back. "I'm not involved with anything. So he's dead?"

Cavanaugh nodded.

Sarge had a hunch that Kevin knew he was dead.

Kevin clearly didn't seem to care one way or another about the news.

"What can you tell us about him?" Cavanaugh asked. "His name, where he lived, that sort of thing?"

"Don't know much," Kevin said. "His name was Douglas Trueman and he and my father went into some business together back before my dad vanished. After my dad left, dear old Doug tried to take up with my mom. He even lived with us for a while, but my mother was pretty broken. She told me one day when we were alone that Douglas was my real father."

Sarge nodded to that.

"As I told the other detectives here, my mother killed herself when I was sixteen and good old Douglas vanished as well, leaving me to clean up the mess, sell my parents house and things, and be on my own. Never saw the bastard again and never want to. Glad they are all gone, actually. I'm starting to get some counseling finally and might actually be able to do a little something before I get too old."

Sarge had no idea if the guy was lying or not, but it was a convincing story. A story he would have been expected to tell.

At least they had a name they could go on for that body in the basement.

"So what's this crime you are suspecting me of being involved with?" Kevin asked.

"We weren't sure if you were involved with your biological father or not," Cavanaugh said. "Sounds like you were not."

"Never saw the guy again after mom died," Kevin said, shrugging. "Never cared to, either."

"Do you know if Douglas had any other family at all?" Cavanaugh asked, glancing at his notes.

Kevin shook his head. "Nope. Not a clue."

They thanked him and they headed back through the hallway and into the noise of the casino.

On the way out, Pickett said, "Cavanaugh, you didn't hear this."

"Hear what?" Cavanaugh asked.

"Exactly," Pickett said as she took out her phone and called Robin.

"We just left Kevin and I cloned his phone," Pickett said to Robin. "Sending it to you now. We rattled his cage pretty well, so if he's involved, he's going to be making some calls."

Pickett nodded and clicked off her phone.

"She's got it."

"You know that I am pretty sure that's illegal," Cavanaugh said, laughing as they got to the front of the casino to get their car from valet parking.

"So is doing what those perverts did to those girls for the last thirty-five years," Pickett said. "Not counting the murders in the first place."

Sarge laughed and patted Cavanaugh on the back. "Don't worry, if anything comes of it, we'll back it up with a legal path to the information."

Cavanaugh laughed as well. "I know. Just enjoying watching you three work is all. No wonder you figure out so many cases."

"We cheat," Pickett said.

"No," Sarge said, "we use modern resources."

"Actually," Cavanaugh said, "you are smarter than the crooks."

"I think I'll take that as a compliment," Sarge said, laughing.

"Don't let it go to your head," Cavanaugh said.

TWENTY-FIVE

June 15th, 2017
Las Vegas, Nevada

PICKETT WAS FIFTY-FIFTY on the odds that Kevin was involved. Part of her wanted him to not be, but part of her knew that the fruit didn't fall far from the tree. And his answers were too pat and expected.

And he had been sixteen when his mother killed herself. He had been old enough to participate in his father's habits and who knows, as a strong boy, what he was forcing his mother to do. Nothing was going to surprise Pickett anymore about this case.

The three of them talked about the theory that Douglas Trueman, if that was his real name, had murdered Cathy Wendt's real father in 1981, when he vanished.

But if he had been dead, who killed those girls and why?

So Pickett was conflicted about that as well. None of them were sure that Cathy Wendt's real father just didn't change his name and keep going.

And he might be alive out there somewhere now.

The afternoon had grown hot when they pulled back up beside Cavanaugh's car in the Bellagio's main parking lot. Right at that moment, Robin called them.

Pickett put it on speakerphone and told Robin that all three of them were still here.

"This gets worse," Robin said.

"I really, really wish you would stop saying that," Cavanaugh said.

"I found Cathy's real father, I think," Robin said. "Kevin called him as soon as you guys left him. The guy's going under the name of Craig C. Verne and he's the right age. We are still digging, but I think he worked as an embalmer from 1999 to 2001. He was licensed. Then he retired, only working those two years. Made a lot of money from somewhere and is still making money."

"Can you get into Kevin's computers and such?" Pickett asked.

"Going to need a warrant for Will and me and our people to try that," Robin said. "The guy might be protected from all sides since the dark web stuff these places were doing was very upscale."

Cavanaugh nodded, then said, "I'll have one for you in thirty minutes. Need a solid reason why, however."

"Suspicion of involvement with twenty-four murders," Robin said.

"Not all thirty-one?" Pickett asked.

Sarge just shook his head.

"Don't say it," Cavanaugh said from the back seat.

"Sorry," Robin said, "but there is another pattern of twenty-four girls going missing, eighteen years old to twenty-two. All brunettes this time, all thin and beautiful. All during the two years that Verne worked as an embalmer."

"Find the goddamned houses they are using," Cavanaugh said. "I'll have the warrant to you as fast as I can."

Pickett had jumped to the exact same conclusion. There were more of these houses out there with dead girls in them. Robin had been right about this getting worse.

A whole bunch worse.

"Will do," Robin said and hung up.

"What do you want us to do?" Pickett asked as Cavanaugh started to climb out.

"Get some rest for the afternoon, some good dinner," Cavanaugh said.

"So we're going out tonight?" Sarge asked.

"It's a date," Cavanaugh said. "Only no dancing. You remember stakeouts from your time on the active list? Or do I need to explain them to you?"

Pickett laughed. She remembered them well. Never had liked them, but oh, did she remember the many nights she and Robin had spent on stakeouts.

"We'll use this car," Cavanaugh said. "Might want to toss some pillows and blankets in here and in the back so we can take turns napping."

"Will do," Pickett said.

Cavanaugh got out, his phone against his ear before he even closed the door.

"Any idea who we are going to be staking out?" Pickett asked.

Sarge just shrugged. "Got a hunch that will depend on what Robin finds with those warrants."

Pickett knew that was right.

"Our first stakeout together," Sarge said, smiling at Pickett.

"Too bad we're going to have a chaperone," Pickett said.

"Well, detective, I am shocked at the very suggestion," Sarge said, laughing.

"I'm shocked you didn't suggest it," Pickett said, getting the car in motion.

"Maybe we can get Cavanaugh to take a break for dinner," Sarge said.

"Now that idea I like," Pickett said.

She would have kissed the man she loved at that moment, but she was already driving.

PART FOUR
Disappointing

TWENTY-SIX

June 15th, 2017
Las Vegas, Nevada

SARGE WAS FEELING full, but not full enough to stay away from seconds.

That afternoon, he and Pickett had gone home, taken a long nap together, then they had showered and put on their most comfortable clothes for the possibly long night ahead. Both had on jeans, light shirts, and tennis shoes.

They both had grabbed light coats as well as the jackets they normally wore over the guns and badges, just in case the night got really cold, which it often did, even in the early summer.

They had filled up the car with gas, bought a bunch of snacks for the night, and filled the cooler with bottles of iced tea and coffee drinks, as well as water and juices.

While they were doing that, they both told their worst stakeout stories. Both of them hoped tonight would not rank in the even memorable ones, except maybe that it would be their very last. Stakeouts

were for active detectives, not retired detectives.

In most cases.

Then they had headed to the Golden Nugget buffet just because it was easy and comfortable and they could wait there until pretty late for Cavanaugh to call.

By the time they got there the dinner rush was over and most of the tourists were on one side of the restaurant by the pool windows. Sarge and Pickett got their normal table clear on the other side of the restaurant and settled in.

The light in there at night was very different from morning. It had a golden glow to it in the seating areas because of large wooden-framed chandeliers, with white light around the buffet area making the area seem like the Promised Land.

Sarge had just finished his first plate of salad and prime rib and some shrimp when Robin called.

Since they were far enough away from any occupied table or server, they put her on speakerphone, turned the sound down a little, and leaned in so they could both hear.

"Both here," Pickett said. "Finishing dinner at the Nugget."

"You two ever get tired of that place?" Robin asked, laughing.

"Tough to get tired of great food, comfortable seating, and nice wait staff," Sarge said.

"Got a point there," Robin said. "Well, we got a hit on about six sets of fingerprints of the customers in the houses. We are pretty sure they are customers because they all live on the East Coast. Two work in the Federal government, which is why we found their prints."

Sarge just shook his head and hoped the worst for them.

Robin went on. "You will never guess who owns five more houses similar to the ones we found earlier in style and shape," Robin said. "Our dear old Ben."

Sarge sat back and looked at Pickett, who looked as surprised as he felt.

"Any direct connection this time?" Pickett asked.

"Again, nothing," Robin said. "He bought them all in 1998, sold them in 1999."

"Did you track Ben's broker on those?" Sarge asked.

"Guy is dead, company out of business since 2005," Robin said. "I pulled up the paperwork that was filed and it looks fine, only the house sales were never finalized and transferred out of Ben's name. Just as the other six."

"Could he be doing this to protect himself?" Sarge asked.

He had believed Ben and Cathy. But that doesn't mean he hadn't been wrong.

"He might be," Robin said. "But I have dug into their accounts, including five corporations they own and control. All money seems to be aboveboard. If they are involved, they are not doing it for the money. Or the money is going somewhere I can't yet find, some off-shore corporation or something."

"So we have found the houses?" Pickett asked.

"Cavanaugh has detectives on all five of them," Robin said. "But we don't want to move on any of them until we find the people behind this sickness and murders."

Sarge suddenly had an idea that had not occurred to him, since before they were dealing with very old houses. But if they were correct and these new houses fired up at the start of this century, they might have some technology in them.

"Robin," Sarge said. "Any way you can get a scan to catch any kind of remote signal coming out of those houses? Like secret taping or monitoring devices broadcasting a signal?"

"Shit," Robin said. "Great idea. "Call you back after I get that going. Not sure why I didn't think of that. Shit."

She hung up.

Pickett smiled at him and pointed to the dessert area of the buffet.

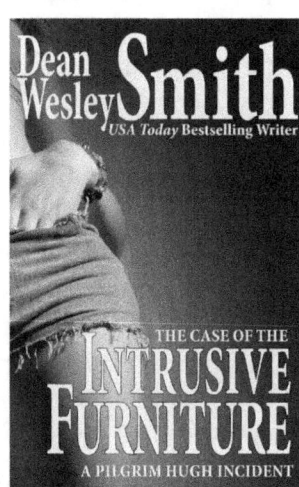

Three Pilgrim Hugh Incidents
Available at your favorite booksellers.

"Nope, not yet. Got a hunch we have time, so I'm going for some more shrimp and a slice of that ham."

Pickett followed him and got a slice of prime rib and some melon balls for her seconds.

And he had been right, they had more than enough time to have seconds, drink a cup of coffee, and get some dessert.

TWENTY-SEVEN

June 15th, 2017
Las Vegas, Nevada

IT WAS JUST after nine in the evening when Robin called back. Most of the buffet was empty and it would close at ten. So Pickett was glad that they still had a little time and their waitress had told them they could stay as long as they wanted, the kitchen staff just had to clean up the food at ten.

Pickett figured it was better sitting here than in a car any longer than they had to.

Pickett put Robin on speakerphone again.

"Cavanaugh got a surveillance warrant for all five houses," Robin said, "and Will has his people set up on all five. They are getting some pretty nasty stuff from four of the five houses, from what Will tells me."

"Sick stuff?" Pickett asked, afraid of the answer.

"Real sick," Robin said. "I warned Will what might be going on. He said he thinks he can keep his people from killing anyone in the house. But after a few minutes they all have stopped watching the feed. They are just recording it."

Pickett understood that perfectly and Sarge just nodded. Her imagination was more than enough to imagine the horror in those houses. She certainly didn't want to see it.

"We are making progress on cracking the web side of this," Robin said. "Pretty clear it is coming from Kevin."

Pickett wasn't surprised at that at all.

"So got any idea why Cavanaugh wants us on this stakeout tonight?" Sarge asked.

"Because he believes," Robin said, "that everyone involved is about ready to cut and run since we have gotten this close. And he hopes to wrap this up before the rats scatter to the trash heaps."

"You got both the father and son locked down, right?" Pickett said.

"They are meeting at midnight tonight." Robin said. "We have trackers on their cars and both of their phones cloned. You shook the kid's tree nicely this afternoon."

Pickett smiled. "That was all Cavanaugh. He can do that to a person if he wants. And in a nice way while at it."

Robin laughed, then went on. "We also just learned about thirty minutes ago from the lab that the guy in the basement, Kevin's biological father, didn't die of natural causes and dehydration. He was poisoned."

That surprised Pickett. The guy just looked like he had sat there and died. They were such a long way in this case from how they started when they saw that body the first time.

"So they cut those early six houses and were waiting for them to be discovered is all," Sarge said. "We just happened to stumble into it all."

"Seems that way," Robin said.

"What wonderful luck," Pickett said.

"Yeah, luck," Sarge said, shaking his head.

"But there is someone else involved, isn't there?" Pickett asked Robin.

"We don't know for sure," Robin said. "But Cavanaugh is guessing that Ben and Cathy are. So he wants you three sitting on them tonight."

Pickett glanced up at the puzzled look on Sarge's face. Then she asked, "What makes Cavanaugh think that?"

"First off, your idea about the cars. We matched a few cash withdrawals from Ben and Cathy's personal accounts for travel to the price of the cars when they were bought. Seems the cars were never used, just put there for show."

"Extremely circumstantial," Pickett said. "But makes sense."

She didn't like it, but it made sense to compare across like that.

"The coincidence of the new five houses being in Ben's name," Robin said, "is another factor. And he did another book of nudes in 2000 called *Brunettes*. Seems like too pat a story to not be checked out."

Now Available
**from all your favorite booksellers
in trade paper and electronic editions**.

DEAN WESLEY SMITH
USA TODAY BESTSELLING AUTHOR

THE LIFE
AND TIMES OF
BUFFALO
JIMMY
★HEADED WEST★

"I agree," Pickett said. "But I sure hope we are wrong."

"I hope so too," Sarge said. "But the cycle of abuse tends to go down through the generations until broken. We all know that."

"Oh, god, tell me Ben and Cathy had no children," Pickett said. "And Kevin has no children."

"They had no children," Robin said.

Pickett was relieved to hear that. No matter what happened tonight, that chain of sickness was broken. Now she just hoped that Cathy and Ben were not a part of all this.

But it was only a hope.

She had nothing else to go on because their story said things were one way, but the facts seemed to be pushing another.

It was going to be a long night.

TWENTY-EIGHT

June 15th, 2017
Las Vegas, Nevada

CAVANAUGH HAD MET them in a twenty-four-hour grocery store parking lot about a block from one of the houses being staked out. It was ten in the evening and he looked actually cheerful as he got out of his car and locked it and climbed into the back of Pickett's SUV.

Sarge glanced at Pickett, who was behind the wheel, and then turned around to Cavanaugh. "Too much caffeine?"

Cavanaugh laughed. "Nope, by tomorrow we'll have this sick case wrapped up and I will only have fourteen days left."

Pickett and Sarge both laughed.

"So where to?" Pickett asked.

"There is a service station about three-quarters of a mile below Cathy and Ben's house, on that crossroads there. They are open twenty-four seven and we can park beside it without being seen much from the highway."

"What happens if they go another way out of the house on the highway?"

"I got a guy with a scope on their garage and driveway," Cavanaugh said. "We'll track them if they leave."

Pickett got the car headed out toward Ben and Cathy's place.

"You believe they are involved?"

"I'm damn hoping not," Cavanaugh said. "But her dad and her brother are meeting tonight at midnight in the one house that is not being used by a customer at the moment. We think this is either a normal meeting or a called meeting."

"Robin or Will or their crew find any sign that either the father or the brother had contacted Ben or Cathy in any way?"

"No," Cavanaugh said. "That's what gives me hope. Unless this is just a regular meeting. On the dark web booking of this stuff, Will's people discovered that two nights a month are left reserved in one house or another. Tonight is one of those nights."

"So we have no idea at all if Ben and Cathy are involved," Sarge said.

"Not a bit that will stand up in any court," Cavanaugh said. "But no matter if Ben and Cathy come out or not, this operation stops tonight. And we toss everyone we can round up into general population and pass the word about exactly what they were doing."

Sarge really liked that idea.

Pickett just laughed, and Sarge could tell she liked it as well.

Thirty minutes later Pickett got the SUV backed into a place in the shadows of the service station lighting, against one side of the building and to the back. They had a clear view of the highway in both directions from there, but Sarge was pretty sure the car didn't look obvious in any way.

"This is stakeout heaven," Pickett said. "Hot coffee in there, bathrooms on the other side of the building."

"We are too damned old to do a regular stakeout," Cavanaugh said.

"I thought you said you weren't old yet," Sarge said.

Cavanaugh waved his hand in dismissal. "I'm just watching out for my senior friends is all."

Pickett actually laughed and Sarge just shook his head. Actually, in real age, Pickett was younger than both he and Cavanaugh.

"I'm going to go tell the guy behind the counter we are here," Cavanaugh said, "so we don't spook him."

"What's the cover story?" Sarge asked.

"Watching for a truckload of stolen watches coming down from the north," Cavanaugh said.

Sarge laughed at that. Maybe this wasn't going to be such a long night after all.

TWENTY-NINE

June 15th, 2017
Las Vegas, Nevada

ALL THREE OF them were munching on some rather tasty fresh donuts that had just been delivered to the service station. Pickett had her favorite, a maple bar, covered completely in maple and still slightly warm, with the maple frosting running so that she had more of it on her face than in her mouth after the first bite.

But she didn't care. It tasted heavenly.

Fresh donuts on a stakeout always did.

It was eleven thirty and they had been there for over an hour and were just getting settled in. They had all decided that the outcome they wanted was to sit there until just before dawn and then go in and help in the raid on those homes.

They had all clearly liked Cathy and Ben.

Suddenly the two-way radio Cavanaugh had with him crackled to life.

"White Lexus SUV pulling out of the garage and heading down the driveway."

"Shit, shit, shit," Cavanaugh said.

Pickett felt exactly the same way.

Sarge just sat shaking his head.

"Tell us which way it turns on the main highway," Cavanaugh said to his spotter.

"Copy," the spotter said.

"And stay in place until dawn, make sure a second car doesn't leave."

"Understood," the cop on the other side said.

Pickett had so hoped that Ben and Cathy were not involved. But it was looking like they were. Or at least Ben was.

She cleaned up her hands and face and put what was left of her maple bar in a bag with Sarge's half-eaten glazed donut.

Sarge put the bag on the floor at his feet.

"Turning toward you on the highway," the spotter said. "White Lexus and I only see one person inside."

"Understood," Cavanaugh said. "We'll pick it up from here."

He then radioed into dispatch that he was going to need some backup on a tail of a white Lexus.

Then they sat in silence, waiting.

"Here it comes," Sarge said.

As the Lexus went by in front of them in the lights from the service station, it was clear who was driving.

Cathy.

Not Ben.

Cathy.

And from what Pickett could tell, it didn't look like Ben was in the car with her.

"Well ain't that a kick," Cavanaugh said as Pickett waited a moment for Cathy to get far enough past, then started up her car and pulled out on the highway.

Pickett wasn't sure what she thought. One thing was for sure, that was not what she had hoped for.

But she knew, knowing just a little of the abuse that Cathy had suffered, it was what she should have expected.

PART FIVE
Unexpected But No Surprise

THIRTY

June 15th, 2017
Las Vegas, Nevada

SARGE SAT IN the passenger seat, helping Pickett keep an eye on the white Lexus a quarter mile in front of them.

Two other unmarked police spotters were leapfrogging them, keeping them informed on a private channel of the location of the Lexus.

They rode in a heavy quiet, almost like it was a funeral. Sarge knew they were all hoping that Cathy would just pull into a grocery store, get some medicine or food and head home.

Sarge knew that was what he was hoping for at least.

None of them wanted her to go to that house with the dead girls on the beds and two buried in the basement.

But after all the years on the force, his detective mind told him he was just kidding himself. Cathy was going right where they knew she was going.

It was clear now that almost from the start in 1977 as a young girl, she had played Ben and helped her father and her brother's father get rich off of not cremating dead people. Then, in 1981, they had killed those girls and set up an entire new business.

And then killed another group in 2001.

Clearly tonight was not a special meeting, but a normal one of the three of them.

"Both men are en route," a dispatcher said to Cavanaugh.

"Make sure all surveillance vehicles on the house are pulled back and out of sight," Cavanaugh said.

"So what's the plan?" Pickett asked of Cavanaugh as Cathy turned toward the house.

"We let all three get inside," Cavanaugh said. "We have the house completely monitored, so as soon as we get enough information from them, we go in and shut it down."

"You have teams on the other four houses?" Sarge asked.

Cavanaugh nodded. "Ready for my signal. In three of them there is a single guy, in another there is a couple from Indiana."

"A couple?" Pickett asked, glancing back at Cavanaugh.

"Afraid so," Cavanaugh said, clearly sounding disgusted.

"How in the hell does a couple bond over sexually abusing long-dead corpses?" Sarge asked, feeling like he wanted to be just sick.

"They met at a funeral?" Pickett asked. "Standing over the corpse viewing. A real romance meet cute if you ask me."

Sarge shook his head and smiled.

Cavanaugh chuckled.

"Maybe they both like to pretend to be vampires," Cavanaugh said. "I hear kids like that sort of thing these days."

"Pretty sure mummified dead bodies don't have blood," Pickett said, laughing.

"Can you imagine the dinner conversations?" Sarge asked. "Honey, you up for some necrophilia this weekend?"

Cavanaugh snorted.

"What would foreplay be like?" Pickett asked. "You play dead so I can get warmed up?"

All three of them laughed and Sarge waved his hand to stop the conversation.

At that point Pickett pulled over into a driveway of a neighbor's house about a block away and shut off the car and lights.

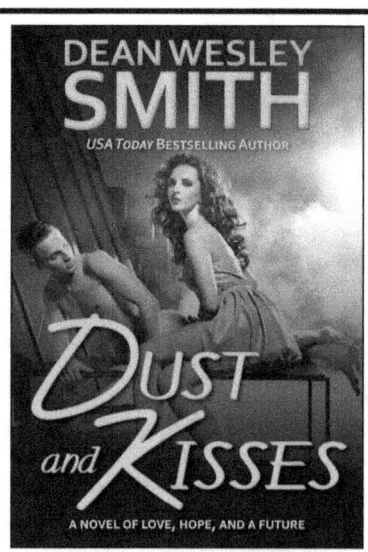

Now Available
from all your favorite booksellers
in trade paper and electronic editions.

"Suspect you were following is entering the building," Cavanaugh's radio reported.

"Both other suspects have just pulled up in front."

A minute later the report came in. "All three suspects are in the building."

"Shall we go to the surveillance van?" Sarge said.

Sarge was not at all sure he wanted to and he could see that Pickett didn't want to either.

He was about to say no when the spotter on the States' home said, "Cavanaugh, another car is leaving the garage. A second white Lexus SUV."

"What the hell is Ben doing?" Sarge asked.

"Damn it," Cavanaugh said.

"We'll go back and pick him up," Pickett said. "You take care of this mess here."

Cavanaugh reported back to the spotter that he needed to report which way the Lexus was headed out of the driveway. Then he called in to headquarters the situation and that they had undercover officers who would be tailing the Lexus and who would need help.

Headquarters responded back in the affirmative and Cavanaugh handed Sarge his radio. "I'll be monitoring the situation from here."

He climbed out and Pickett got the car headed back toward the States' house.

"What in the world is Ben doing?" Pickett asked.

"Maybe they both are involved," Sarge said. "No way of knowing."

"Get Robin on the phone, tell her what is happening," Pickett said. "We might need her to track Ben's car if we lose him."

Sarge nodded, put Cavanaugh's radio between his legs and called Robin on the phone. He put her on speakerphone and they filled her in on what was happening.

"Nothing is going on at the moment in the house," Robin said. "I am getting the live feed just as the police are. They are all sitting in the living room talking. Like a board of director's meeting or something."

Sarge just shook his head. In that house there were three girls in three beds, all dead since 2001. The mummified bodies embalmed and adjusted for sex. And two other girls were buried in the basement, ready to be dug up for sex. And those three just sat in the living room talking.

"Can you hear what they are saying?"

"She is telling them about your visit," Robin said. "She is laughing at you guys for being fooled."

Sarge looked at Pickett as she was driving. The woman he loved looked angry.

Very angry.

And he felt the same way.

"Detectives," the spotter Cavanaugh had watching the States' home said.

"Go ahead," Sarge said.

"The second Lexus turned toward town as well. One person inside."

"Thank you," Sarge said. "Stay in position."

"Understand, sir," the spotter said.

Sarge then said, "Cavanaugh."

"Go ahead," Cavanaugh said.

"We're going to try to intercept the second Lexus about three miles in on the highway and will follow it."

"Understood," Cavanaugh said.

"First time in a long time that I wished I had police lights on this thing," Pickett said.

Sarge laughed. "Chief gave us our guns and badges. Let's don't go hoping for too much."

She laughed, but never took her eyes off the road as she expertly worked her way through traffic, not even really speeding.

She was a great driver. Of that there was no doubt.

THIRTY-ONE

June 16th, 2017
Las Vegas, Nevada

IT WAS ONLY a few minutes after midnight as Pickett swung across the highway into a convenience store parking lot and turned the car quickly around.

If she had timed it right and the second Lexus hadn't turned off, it would be passing this point in about one minute.

If he had turned off, it was going to take luck and some of Robin's skills to find it.

While they had been driving, Robin had been not only reporting a little on the meeting in the house over Sarge's phone, but had been trying to hack a GPS system to track the second Lexus.

"Got it," Robin said after a moment. "Coming at your position in thirty seconds."

"Thanks," Pickett said. "Stick with us, we're going to hang back some and try to not spook the driver."

At that moment a white Lexus SUV went past in front of them.

Ben was driving.

Pickett took her time pulling into traffic behind him. Since Robin had him tracking on GPS, they could take a few more chances. And that was a relief.

"Cavanaugh," Sarge said into the radio.

"Go ahead," Cavanaugh said.

"We have picked up Ben driving the second car, heading into town."

"Good work," Cavanaugh said. "Stay on him. Let us know if he is coming this way."

"Understood," Sarge said.

"I'm betting he's not," Robin said. "I've been listening to the conversation and Cathy was bragging about how she had put on a show for Ben in front of the police."

"So where is Ben heading?" Pickett asked.

Sarge shook his head. "He was a man totally in love with Cathy and willing to overlook a lot."

Pickett nodded to that. She had sensed the same thing about Ben, which was why she was hoping Cathy and Ben weren't involved.

"My sense," Sarge said, "is that our visit forced him to put two and two together and finally decide he can't deal with anymore. He's not going to join them. Maybe he's headed for the airport to leave her."

Pickett nodded. That made perfect sense.

"Or he's going to jump onto the freeway and just head to California," Sarge said.

Pickett nodded to that as well. "If he starts to do that, we're going to need the state police to stop and arrest him before he gets to the border."

"Let's see where he's headed first," Sarge said. "There might be something else going on here."

Pickett nodded.

Sarge laughed. "With this case, I think that's the norm, not the unusual."

Pickett agreed with that completely. So far they had been totally wrong about Cathy. There was a very good chance they were wrong about Ben on this as well.

They were soon going to know. More than likely in two more stoplights.

"How is the meeting going?" Sarge asked Robin.

"Kevin is telling his part of the story about his meetings with you two and then the three of you," Robin said.

At that point, Ben in the Lexus in front of them hit the stoplight. A right turn would take him to the airport or the freeway out of town. A left turn would take him in the direction of the house.

He went straight instead.

"Not a clue what he is doing," Sarge said.

They followed him for another ten minutes until finally the white Lexus pulled into the parking lot of Love Lost Mortuary and Crematorium.

"Damn it all to hell," Sarge said.

"I am pulling up security cameras on the place," Robin said. "I'll forward them to your phone, Pickett. Sarge, you keep your phone open on speaker."

"Understood," Sarge said.

He really liked how the three of them worked as a team and tonight the team-work was proving invaluable.

Pickett got parked just a half block down the street from the mortuary and the car shut down. At that moment her phone beeped and she clicked it on.

She showed Sarge the images that Robin was forwarding.

Ben had climbed out of his car and had gone to the back door and was unlocking it.

"Do they own this thing?" Sarge asked.

"Got two of Will's people digging right now," Robin said.

Pickett watched as Ben went inside and the image on her phone switched to a camera inside to follow him.

"Cavanaugh?" Sarge said into the police radio.

"Go ahead," Cavanaugh said.

"Ben has stopped at a mortuary and crematorium and has entered it."

"What?" Cavanaugh said.

Pickett smiled as Sarge gave him the address. Then Sarge said, "We need an instant warrant for Robin to tap the security feed."

"Understood," Cavanaugh said. "You need backup?"

"Not yet," Sarge said. "We are just standing off and observing."

Cavanaugh signed off with a promise he would have the warrant at light speed.

Pickett just shook her head as Robin said, "Thank you."

"Stupid active cases have so many rules," Sarge said, grinning at Pickett.

Then they watched as Ben went into the crematorium part of the building and went through a procedure to heat up the ovens.

"Shit, he's going to cremate a body," Pickett said after watching for a moment.

"But what body?" Sarge asked.

Pickett had no response to that one. She had no idea.

THIRTY-TWO

June 16th, 2017
Las Vegas, Nevada

SARGE KNEW IT took time to heat up the ovens to a temperature that would cremate a human body. And then the procedure took some time as well.

Ben went over to a chair against one wall, sat down, and picked up a magazine that was there on an end table and started to read.

Sarge was amazed that the guy seemed like he was in no hurry at all. He and his wife had no idea that they were surrounded by police.

And clearly Ben had done this before. He seemed comfortable with the procedure.

But Sarge still couldn't begin to figure out who Ben planned to cremate.

The warrant came through after only five minutes. Cavanaugh was right, it was light speed.

"I have trimmed off all the images I got from before the exact moment of the warrant," Robin said.

"Good work, partner," Pickett said. "What's happening at the house?"

"They are still talking money and business and websites and you name it," Robin said. "Going to be ugly for them in court because they actually talked about the damage one client had done to one of the bodies he dug up and how that had to be 'repaired' for the next client."

"Besides disgusting, how bad can we get all the clients on this?"

"Class D felonies," Robin said.

Sarge nodded. "Abuse of a corpse is usually a misdemeanor, but when sex is involved it becomes a felony. A sexual crime that can't be dropped from a record and is up to four years in jail per infraction."

Pickett looked at him with a puzzled look.

"Had a really nasty case about three years before I retired," Sarge said, smiling. "A guy killed his wife because she wouldn't have sex with him, then he kept her body around for a week, forcing himself on the body."

"Oh, yuck," Pickett said.

"The crap we have all seen," Robin said.

"This case ranks right up there on the crap meter," Sarge said.

Pickett could only agree with that.

"Looks like we might just be heading into new lands of crap on Cavanaugh's end," Robin said. "Cathy just asked her father and brother if they wanted to go have a little fun."

"How far will Cavanaugh let that go?" Pickett asked.

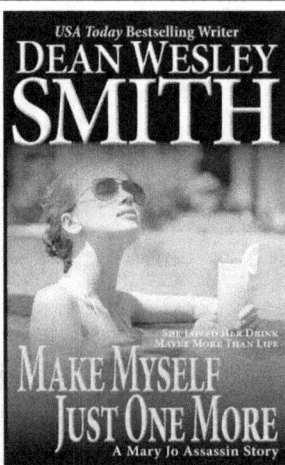

Three Mary Jo Assassin Stories
Available at your favorite booksellers.

Sarge really didn't want to think about it and was very glad they weren't watching.

"As far as it takes to make sure no jury seeing the film would ever let them go," Robin said.

At that moment Ben glanced at his watch and stood and headed for the door.

Robin jumped the security cams to follow him until Ben got a rolling table to put a body on. Then he went back out to his car and opened the back.

"Holy shit, he has a body in there," Pickett said.

"Cavanaugh," Sarge said into the radio. "Send backup quietly. Ben has a body and is loading it onto a cart to cremate. We're going to need to stop him."

"Be damned careful," Cavanaugh said.

Sarge checked his gun and Pickett did the same.

They both stripped off their jackets so their badges were in plain sight.

Then they studied the image on Pickett's phone. Ben had managed to get a body out of the back of the SUV and loaded on the cart. It looked like a small woman's body.

He got the back door of the mortuary open again and went in, pushing the cart. He didn't seem to be concerned about being caught, from what Sarge could tell. This guy clearly must have done this a bunch of times, that was for sure.

"We don't dare wait for backup," Pickett said.

"Let's go," Sarge said, nodding.

"Cavanaugh," Sarge said into the radio, "tell the backup arriving that there are two detectives on the scene and in the building."

"Copy," Cavanaugh said.

Sarge put the radio on the seat.

Pickett nodded and they both climbed out, closing their doors slowly and quietly. The evening air was still warm from the day and the sounds of the neighborhood were only a dog barking and a car without a muffler in the distance.

This was not something he had expected to be doing tonight.

Or actually any night ever again.

But they simply had no choice.

THIRTY-THREE

June 16th, 2017
Las Vegas, Nevada

PICKETT COULD FEEL the adrenaline rushing through her system as they quickly ran around to the back of the building. She had her phone with the security images still streaming to it and Robin was on Sarge's phone. But at the moment both phones were in their pockets and their guns were in their hands.

The back door had closed behind Ben and Sarge carefully tested it.

"Locked," he whispered.

He took out his phone. "Robin, are the locks part of the security system?"

Sarge said, "Thanks," and put the phone back in his pocket.

"Nope," he said to Pickett.

They both still carried their lock pick kits with them and Sarge bent down quickly by the door while Pickett watched the security feed.

"Ben's reached the cremation room," Pickett said, watching the video feed on her phone. If he went right to the oven with the body, they were going to need to hurry otherwise the body was going to be damaged and hard to identify.

Sarge quickly worked at the lock. Of the two of them, he was the fastest at picking locks and from the looks of it, the security lock on the mortuary would take him about a minute at best.

As she watched the security feed of Ben, he uncovered the body and took it out of the body bag.

It was a woman, looked to be around thirty, who had been embalmed and clearly been dead for a while and left in a dry, open place. Maybe over a year from the looks of the stage of mummification. Pickett didn't want to think about where this woman had been kept.

Or for what reason.

But as she watched, she realized she was going to get to see real quickly what the woman was being used for since Ben was also undressing.

"Oh, please hurry," Pickett said to Sarge.

"Why?" Sarge asked, not stopping his work on the door lock.

"Because Ben is about to have sex with the dead woman before he cremates her."

That stopped Sarge and he looked up at Pickett. "You are kidding me?"

"I am not," Pickett said.

She watched the image as Ben took off his clothes and moved toward the corpse.

"Any sign of a gun?" Sarge asked, working on the door.

"He's naked and about ten feet from his clothes," Pickett said. "The only thing he's armed with is disgusting."

Sarge laughed as he clicked open the door and stood.

At that moment two officers came around the building.

"Detectives Pickett and Carson," Pickett said to the cops in a loud whisper,

showing them her badge. One cop was a man, the other a woman, and both looked young. In the faint light of the parking lot Pickett couldn't see their names.

"Follow us in," Sarge said. "We got a suspect in the crematorium with a body."

Both cops nodded.

"We don't think he is armed, but we take no chances," Sarge said.

Both nodded again.

Sarge went through the door first and went to the right while Pickett followed and went left.

The two cops followed, moving quietly as well, one stopping for a second to brace open the door.

Sarge took out his phone. "Robin, anything we should be worried about?"

"You are clear all the way to the event," Robin said. "Turn right into the hallway ahead and go about fifty paces to the door on the left."

He put the phone back in his pocket. "Robin says we are clear."

Pickett nodded, staring at the image over her phone. "Things are getting heated in the crematorium."

Sarge laughed and headed off, gun drawn, but down.

Pickett smiled at the two cops, then followed Sarge, her gun in one hand, the phone in the other. The two new cops were in for a story tonight that she was fairly certain they would never tell their children.

They made quick time in formation, as they had all been trained, down the hallway.

They spread out on both sides of the door to the crematorium.

Then Sarge carefully tried the door and discovered it was unlocked.

He held up one finger, then two, then three, and he went in first.

Pickett had the phone put away in her pocket and she went in beside Sarge.

The two cops came in behind them and went either direction along the wall.

The room smelled hot from the oven fire and had a slight gas tint to the air.

The gurney with the body was smack in the middle of the room, the woman's corpse facing upward.

Ben was facing downward.

Ben looked up from where he was, lying on top of the mummified woman's body. He seemed stunned and a little confused.

"Please get down with your hands in the air," Sarge said, moving to Ben's right.

Pickett, with her gun trained on Ben, went to the left.

The two patrol officers stayed put against the wall near the door.

Ben did as asked, clearly aroused from what he had been doing.

"Lie face down on the floor and put your hands behind your head.

Ben went slowly to his knees, then down to the floor and put his hands behind his head.

"Officer, cuff him please," Sarge said.

The woman officer nodded and came up and put a knee in the middle of Ben's back, pressing him and his erection down against the hard floor, then roughly cuffed him.

"Make sure he doesn't make a move," Pickett said to the young woman officer.

The young officer glanced at the mummified body of the woman on the table, then at Ben on the floor, and said, "He makes a move and I'll step on his dick with my boots."

Pickett and Sarge both laughed as Ben jerked.

Sarge took out his phone and said, "Tell Cavanaugh we are clear here and Ben is in custody."

Sarge nodded, laughed, and put the phone back in his pocket.

"Officer," Sarge said to the guy still beside the door, clearly looking like he was in shock, "please go back to the parking lot and escort the detectives that are arriving in here."

The officer nodded and left, looking very relieved.

"Cavanaugh already knows," Sarge said to Pickett. "And Robin is going to stream the show going on at the other house to your phone. She said it's about to get interesting and they are getting ready to go in."

Pickett pulled out her phone as the image switched.

Kevin and an older man were getting undressed in a bedroom that looked like a master bedroom beside a huge king bed. A corpse of a woman with brunette hair was in the bed, under the covers.

The old guy looked to be almost eighty and starting to get frail.

As the two men finished getting undressed and were standing beside the bed, Cathy came into the room, also naked.

But there was one thing she had with her that no one expected. A very nasty looking pistol with what looked to be a sound suppressor on it.

Robin had streamed the audio as well, so when Cathy came into the room, Pickett heard her say, "Let's really have some fun, shall we?"

Both men nodded.

"Pull back the covers and climb in there with that young woman," Cathy said to the two men.

They did. Her brother had an erection. Her father did not.

The woman was completely mummified and her legs were spread.

"Great," Cathy said. Then she shot her brother once in the head, then her father before he could even move.

Both Pickett and Sarge jumped at that.

Pickett had not seen that coming.

"Holy shit," Sarge said.

"Damn that was fun," Cathy said. "Now I can have some real fun."

She put the gun on the dresser near the door and climbed into the bed with the three bodies. And before Cavanaugh and his men could get there, she was completely covered in blood.

THIRTY-FOUR

June 30th, 2017
Las Vegas, Nevada

FOR THE FIRST four days after all the arrests, the press had kept everything quiet about finding bodies in all the houses. Sarge had been impressed they had held off that long.

As many families as possible had been notified before the press had started to talk about the mess, but even after the first little bit, the press was focusing on helping find families instead of the sensationalism of the entire crimes.

In fact, most of the facts about the sexual ring were kept tight and around the country arrest warrants were being issued for the clients that had used those houses over the last fifteen years.

Ben and Cathy had really helped with that, since all the clients had been recorded and files had been carefully kept by Ben, including photographs.

And, as Cavanaugh had suggested, many of the men arrested had been put into general population of a prison to be held for extradition. It seemed that having sex with the dead bodies of women tended to upset even the most hardened criminals and police officers.

Turned out that many of the clients were not in good enough health after a short time in jail to be extradited. Both Sarge and Pickett found that wonderfully funny.

On the day after the raids, with a search warrant on Ben and Cathy's home, Cavanaugh and the other detectives had also found two more women's bodies in a hidden room in the basement. One was a missing person's woman from about a year ago, the most recent of all the murders.

Sarge was very glad that he and Pickett were off the case after arresting Ben. They had just spent the time relaxing, watching movies, exercising some, and eating far too much.

Ben and Cathy had their pictures splashed all over the newspapers around the country as the "Necrophilia Killers." And Ben's books and art suddenly vanished from art galleries and stores.

He had become famous, but not for his art.

Now, finally, after a pretty good countdown, it was Cavanaugh's last day as an active detective and tomorrow would be his first as an active member of the Cold Poker Gang Task Force.

So Pickett and Sarge were throwing him a party at their place with all the gang coming, and he was also getting a party at the station before he left there.

Cavanaugh had called it a "goodbye–hello" kind of day.

Sarge and Pickett, with the help of Robin and Will, had brought in food and a massive cake. And had even locked the cats in a back bedroom in Pickett's side of the condo just so they wouldn't accidently escape.

Even the Chief of Police was stopping by to officially make Cavanaugh a member of the Gang.

Outside, the evening was warm, but not bad for the middle of the summer. In a few hours they all might be able to actually sit on the balcony upstairs. That balcony had almost a three-hundred-degree view of the entire valley, including right down the Strip. Best view in all of the city as far as Sarge was concerned. The main reason he had bought the condo in the first place.

Robin and Will were upstairs, setting up the cake and the table, and Sarge and Pickett were in the kitchen working on putting out the last of the food trays they had bought.

The condo smelled of fresh bread and deli meats.

Sarge felt they were about ready and it was still a half hour before people would start arriving.

"You know," Pickett said as she finished the last tray of meats, "I can't believe how lucky we are."

"Lucky how?" Sarge said. "You mean how lucky we are to be rich and in this place."

Pickett laughed and said, "Yeah, that too, but lucky to have each other and all these friends we work with."

"I agree," Sarge said, going over to her and hugging her. "What brought that up?"

"All this," Pickett said, "the party, everything. But I was just thinking how lucky I was to still be working as a detective. And working beside the man I love as a partner."

Sarge kissed her again. "I feel the same way."

At that moment there was a knock at the door and Cavanaugh entered. He saw them standing, holding each other in the kitchen, and shook his head.

"Haven't we had enough dead-people sex for one month?"

"Oh, trust me, Cavanaugh," Pickett said, "our sex is far, far from dead."

"What did I just hear?" Robin asked as she came down the stairs toward the kitchen.

"Far, far too much information for my young cars," Cavanaugh said, laughing as Robin went to him for a hug.

Pickett hugged him as well and then Sarge shook his hand. "Congratulations, you made it to the light side."

"The no-paperwork zone," Cavanaugh said, laughing. "It took me most of yesterday just to tell the two young detectives who are taking over that last case what paperwork hadn't been done yet."

"Oh, that's just evil," Pickett said, laughing.

"They'll just do it to other young detectives when they retire," Cavanaugh said.

Sarge just laughed and remembered that he had done the same thing the last day before he had retired as well.

Over the next thirty minutes most of the other fifteen Cold Poker Gang members arrived, some with spouses. And the chief arrived and congratulated Cavanaugh on the transition.

"Welcome aboard the task force," Sarge said to Cavanaugh. "I hope you can play poker and like to lose money."

"I play poker just fine," Cavanaugh said. "But not to lose money. And you guys actually play poker?"

"We do," Pickett said. "Some better than others."

"Just bring enough cash each week," Sarge said, smiling at Cavanaugh. "And you'll fit in just fine."

"And to think I thought this task force would be all fun and games," Cavanaugh said, smiling.

At that everyone laughed and the Cold Poker Gang gained one great new member.

And the food and the drinks and the laughing lasted well into the night. Not bad for a bunch of old retired people.

Coming Next Issue in *Smith's Monthly*

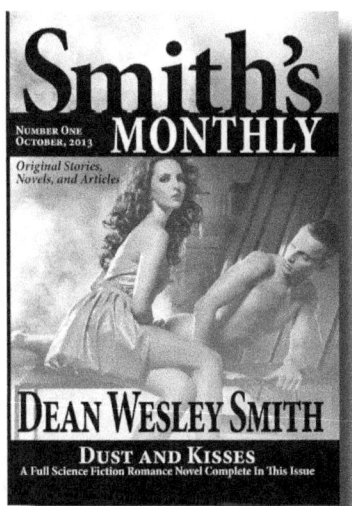

#1...October 2013

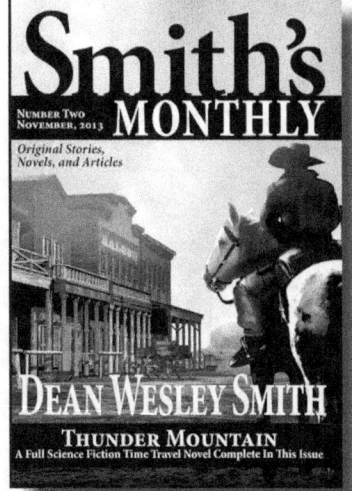

#2...November 2013

#3...December 2013

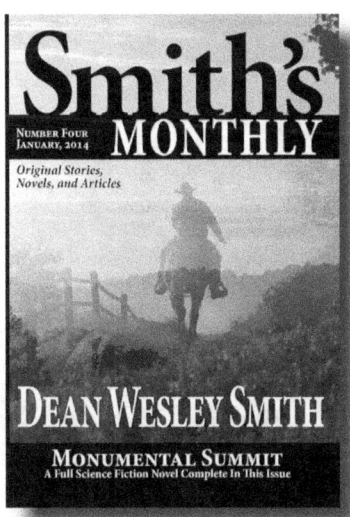

#4...January 2014

#5...February 2014

#6...March 2014

#7...April 2014

#8...May 2014

#9...June 2014

#10...July 2014

#11...August 2014

#12...September 2014

#13...October 2014

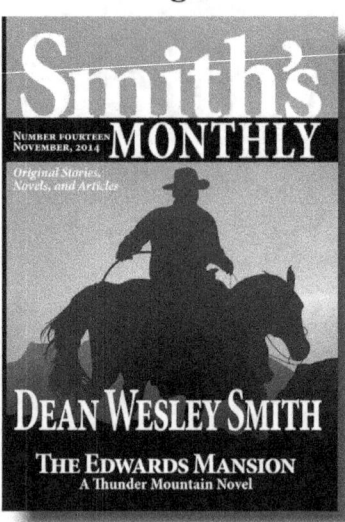

#14...November 2014

#15...December 2014

#16...January 2015

#17...February 2015

#18...March 2015

#19...April 2015

#20...May 2015

#21...June 2015

#22...July 2015

#23...August 2015

#24...September 2015

#25...October 2015

#26...November 2015

#27...December 2015

#28...January 2016

#29...February 2016

#30...March 2016

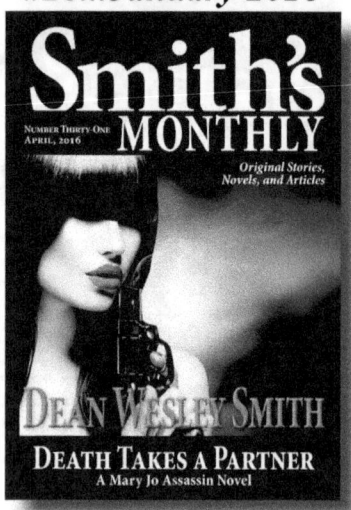

#31...April 2016

#32...May 2016

#33...June 2016

#34...July 2016

#35...August 2016

#36...September 2016

#37...October 2016

#38...November 2016

#39...December 2016

#40...January 2017

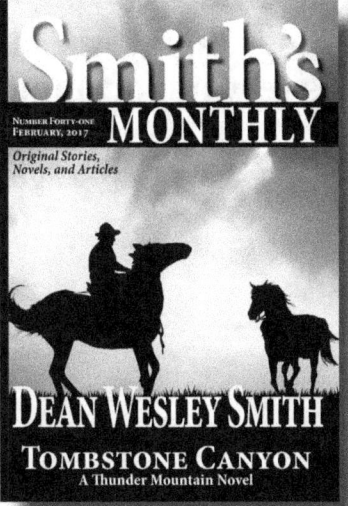

#41...February 2017

#42...March 2017

#43...April 2017

Don't Miss an Issue!

Subscribe

Electronic Subscription:

6 Issues... $29.99

12 Issues... $49.99

Paper Subscription:

6 Issues... $59.99

12 Issues... $99.99

For Full Subscription Information Go To:

www.SmithsMonthly.com

**All Issues Also Available
at Your Favorite Bookstore**

Thank You!!

I would like to thank the following wonderful people who support my blog and my work through Patreon. Your support is very important to me. Thanks!

Irette Y Patterson
Kathryn Rooney
Erick Lindman
Christopher Ridge
Raphael Husbands
James Gotaas
milady133
Danica Oakley
Kenny Norris
Kate MacLeod
Leah Cutter
Leigh Anderson
Robert J. McCarter
Jennette Heikes
Jamie Curierre
Albert Lemke
Marsha Kessler
Diane Darcy
Robin Brande
James Husum
Terry Mixon
Shantnu Tiwari
Chong Go
Maria Grace
Gnondpom
David Hendrickson
Fen

Sherman Cox
Miguel Angel Alonso Pulido
Marian Goldeen
Michelle Tatam
J.R. Murdock
Gunnar Gunderson
Jesse P Thurston
coraa
Martin Barkawitz
David Beers
Leslie Claire Walker
Nancy Hendrickson
F.I. Goldhaber
Michael J Lawrence
Barbara G. Tarn
Anthony St. Clair
Ann Tucker
Karl Gallagher
T. Thorn Coyle
Cristof Jones Harrison
Tasha Turner Lennhoff
Brenda Smith
Kari Wolfe
Mary Jo Rabe

And a very special thank you to Betsey Wilcox.

www.ingramcontent.com/pod-product-compliance
Lightning Source LLC
Chambersburg PA
CBHW081153170626
46813CB00009B/3181